Night Side of Eden

David Barrett-Murrer

dbm Books

For Janice, my wife and lifelong friend.
And, in Loving Memory of Dorothy, Edwin and William Murrer.
We will meet again.

Book Cover, *Transcendence*, by dbm

First Edition 2025

Contents

Prologue

PART ONE

S ophia was intrigued by a man at the bar. His impeccable attire and charming smile exuded an air of mystery. He sat on a stool, leisurely sipping a glass of brandy, his gaze fixed on her. Feeling his attention, Sophia frowned and turned away.

At their small table, her friends were talking about the concert.

'What a show tonight! The music is still buzzing in my head,' Melissa said, sipping her champagne. 'I doubt if Nigel Kennedy could have played the solo violin any better.'

'Fantastic acoustics,' Claire added, puffing on her e-cigarette and looking at her watch. 'Our ride should be here soon. I hope Richard knows where we are.'

'He does,' Melissa said, turning and narrowing her eyes. 'There's a guy at the bar smiling at us. He looks rather dapper.'

Sophia glanced at him, and he waved as if he knew her.

'Do you know him?' Claire asked Sophia.

'I'm not sure. He does look familiar, but I can't place him.' Sophia felt her heart flutter with excitement and some apprehension, and she had to resist the urge to steal another glance at him.

A waiter came over carrying a drink on a silver tray.

'Excuse me, ladies,' he said with a northern accent, facing Sophia. 'The gentleman at the bar asked me to give you this drink. He is Lord Anthony Radcliffe and would like to meet you.'

Sophia glanced briefly at the man. He smiled, and she felt an attraction to him. Taking the cocktail, she made a face with a raised eyebrow at her friends and stood.

'I might as well meet him.' She had been single for several months and enjoyed the thrill of dating new men and women. However, she had yet to find her true love. Of course, Claire, one of her ex-girlfriends, wouldn't be pleased about her meeting this man. After their brief holiday romance in New Orleans during Mardi Gras, which she ended because Claire was too domineering, their friendship had become strained.

'You know our lift will be here soon!' Claire stated loudly. 'Why are you always so impulsive, Sophia?' she added, her voice tinged with annoyance.

'I know, but I want to meet him, and I can always get a taxi back.' She picked up her bag and wandered over to the bar. He stood to greet her and smiled. He was tall, his frame accentuated by a silk-trimmed blue tuxedo and an open-necked white shirt. His close-cropped dark hair was starting to grey at the temples, adding a touch of maturity to his rugged charm, and his brown eyes held a hint of mystery. From the small age lines on his face, she realised he was older than she had first thought, which added a layer of intrigue.

'Thank you for joining me.' He gave her a charming smile. 'I'm certain we met at Ascot. You are Sophia, aren't you?'

'I am, and I was at Ascot this year, but I don't recall meeting you.'

'Strange, because I remember you. Anyway, you look even more enchanting tonight. Did you enjoy the concert?'

'I did, yes. I have always loved Vivaldi's *Four Seasons*.' She sipped her cocktail, savouring the blend of tangy fruit and the warmth of aromatic brandy. 'That is nice. What is it?'

'I had the barman mix you a special. He calls it Blissfulness.'

'It certainly has a kick.' Seeing her friends preparing to leave, she finished the drink and felt quite woozy.

He touched her hand, and she trembled with excitement. There was something intriguing about him—something mysterious and alluring.

'I'm going to a nightclub in the West End if you fancy a bit of fun.' He took out his phone and made a call. 'Brian, I'll be leaving shortly,' he said, then listened and put the phone away. 'Good, my chauffeur will be outside.'

His eyes had a glint of mystery that caught her interest, and she felt a tempting urge to go with him. However, she felt uneasy, concerned that he was a stranger, and she didn't recall meeting him at Ascot.

'I know your father, Sir John,' he said reassuringly. 'We meet frequently at the Masonic Lodge. He likes playing chess, and we've had several challenging games.'

She smiled with relief and glanced back at her friends. Richard had arrived, and Melissa waved her over. She thought about going with them, and then, smiling at Anthony, she decided to have some fun.

'I'm staying, guys,' she told them, picking up her silver shawl from the chair at their table. 'I'll see you tomorrow.'

'Who is he?' Melissa asked.

'One of Daddy's Masonic friends. I think we met at Ascot.'

'I was at Ascot with you and didn't see him there,' Claire said with narrowed eyes. She picked up her bag and shook her head.

'Yeah.' Sophia chuckled. 'But you were wasted most of the time there.'

Claire scowled at her. 'So were you!'

'You take care,' Melissa said, picking up her bag.

Sophia enjoyed Claire's annoyance. 'I'll call you tomorrow,' she said, watching her friends leave with Richard. Then, smiling, she joined Anthony.

'What's this club like?' she asked him.

'You'll love it. Got some great underground bands from the US playing tonight.'

'Let's go.'

Outside, a man in a uniform stood by a blue Range Rover. He nodded to Lord Anthony as they approached, then opened the back passenger door for them. They climbed in, and he closed the door.

As she settled, the chauffeur glanced at her from the driver's seat. He smiled with a raised brow, turned, and drove off.

'Thank you for joining me,' Anthony said with a beaming smile, moving closer to her.

Sophia closed her eyes for a few moments, feeling weak and disoriented. Rubbing her forehead, she wondered if it was the effect of that potent brandy cocktail. Then, looking out the window, she realised they were driving away from the West End, and she felt a chill of concern.

'I've changed my mind. I don't want to go clubbing,' she said, breaking out in a hot sweat. 'I don't feel well. Please stop. I want to go home.'

As she fumbled in her bag for her phone, she noticed Anthony reaching into his jacket pocket and pulling out a small white sponge. Before she could ask what he was doing, he crushed the sponge in his hand, releasing a potent smell that made her nose twitch. Suddenly, Anthony grabbed her and held the sponge firmly over her mouth and nose. The pungent odour numbed her senses. Panic set in as she struggled to push him away, but his strength was too much for her. She felt a wave of dizziness wash over her and slumped, losing consciousness.

Chapter One

Edward, struggling for breath, his heart pounding in his chest and his body throbbing with fatigue, leaned heavily against his front door and fumbled for his keys. This morning's jog around the park near his townhouse in Kensington had left him utterly depleted. Inside, he hung his sweater on the wooden coat stand, caught a glimpse of his reflection in the hall mirror, and let out a weary sigh. At forty-seven, his hair was greying at the temples, and he had fine lines around his eyes and a deeply furrowed brow.

In the double-aspect, teak-panelled study, he slumped into his worn leather recliner and stretched out his aching legs. Yawning, he closed his eyes, took a few slow breaths, and relaxed. As he was drifting to sleep, he heard a young woman calling urgently, 'Help me, please help me, please!' He sat up and looked around, but no one was there. Holding his breath, he realised it was a psychic impression, and a chill ran down his spine. Breathing a heavy sigh, he lay back down and closed his eyes again. It had been years since he had tapped into his psychic ability.

Focusing on the chakras in his body, he connected the Ajna centre in his forehead with the centre in his solar plexus. As the internal chakras aligned, a host of fleeting contacts entered his awareness, and he had to filter out the spurious background impressions. Gradually, he created a calm, psychic sensitivity and waited a long time, focused on the contact before the woman connected with him again.

'Help me... Please, I've been abducted!' She sounded desperate.

'I'm Edward. What's happened?' he asked.

'Edward, Edward Caster! You hear me! Thank God. I've seen your TV shows and been calling you in my mind.'

'Who are you?'

'Sophia. My father is Sir John Henderson. Please contact him.'

'Where are you?'

'I don't know, I—Oh, shit. They're coming for me again, and they use drugs that make me—'

Edward sat up and rubbed his forehead. When Sophia connected, he had the impression that she was imprisoned underground in what seemed to be an old bunker. He made some notes and drew a floor plan of the place in a notebook on his desk.

The study door opened, and his daughter Lucy entered with a tray of tea and biscuits. She placed the tray on the desk, looked at him and frowned.

'You all right, Dad?'

He smiled at her. She had inherited some of his psychic abilities.

'Have you heard of Sophia Henderson?'

'Henderson, Sophia?' She puckered for a moment. 'Yeah, that does ring a bell. She's a socialite. I saw a picture of her in Tatler. She was at Ascot with some boozy friends. Why?'

'Well, I got a psychic buzz from her. She seems to be in trouble.'

She frowned. 'But you stopped that psychic stuff when you finished your TV shows.'

'I did, but she still managed to get through and asked me to contact her dad. Can you do some research on them?'

'Sure, I'll Google them.' She poured a cup of tea and handed it to him.

'You look happy.' He took the cup.

'It's good to see you interested in something. You've been moping around ever since Mum passed away.'

He took a deep breath and, with a sense of nostalgia, thought about Glenda, his wife. 'It's hard to believe it's been two years already,' he said. They had first met at one of his psychic shows in London and were immediately drawn to each other. After a whirlwind romance, they married in Florida during his tour of America. A year later, Lucy was born. 'It's still strange not having her around,' he said and sighed.

'Yeah, but we know Mum's okay. She came to both of us several times after her funeral.'

He nodded, feeling a bite of anger at her killer, who was never caught, while Glenda, his loving companion, was dead. All because he used his psychic ability to help convict a group of terrorists. The car bomb was meant to kill him, but his wife had used the car early that morning instead. The memory surfaced of her calling goodbye to him as she left, and he had experienced a psychic chill. He rushed to the hall, opened the front door, and was hit with the sound and shock wave of the explosion. The image of his dead wife in the burning car was forever etched in his mind.

'Dad!' Lucy nudged him. 'What's this?' She motioned to his drawing of the bunker.

'That's where I sensed the girl was being held. It may be nothing. You know how these psychic impressions can be wrong or misunderstood.'

'Not with you. I'll do the research.' She sat at his desk and used his laptop.

He watched her and smiled. She was now seventeen, a young adult. Her blonde hair was pulled neatly back, and she wore a short blue dress. She had grown up fast since the accident. Occasionally, he sensed his wife overshadowing her but said nothing. Closing his eyes, he recalled some happy times before the car bomb, and drifted asleep.

'Dad.' Lucy woke him.

He yawned, rolled his head, sat up and looked at the wall clock. He had been asleep for two hours.

'Sir John wants you to call him,' she said, stretching her back. 'After a lotta hassle, I got through to him. Initially, he wasn't keen, thought it was a scam, but his wife's an avid fan of your TV shows.' She chuckled. 'I heard her pestering him on the phone, and then she spoke to me. You're right. Their daughter has disappeared.'

She showed him a picture on his laptop. 'That's Sophia on Facebook.'

He viewed a laughing, dark-haired young woman with her thumbs up. She had light-brown eyes that sparkled with mischief, a fair complexion, and ultra-white teeth. There was a caption under the photo: Footloose and fancy-free.

'Are the police involved?'

'Not sure. He didn't want to talk on the phone but gave me a secure number for you to call him.'

'Okay.' He picked up the phone and smiled at her. 'You are an excellent assistant. Well done. I'll have to put you on the payroll.' He could see from her big smile that she liked being his assistant.

He called the number. 'Hi, Sir John? It's Edward Caster.'

'Thank God. I need to see you, Edward. My chauffeur will be with you soon. Your secretary assured me you would come, so I sent Henry over.'

'Okay, I'll be bringing my assistant with me.'

'Fine, time is of the essence, you understand?'

The doorbell rang, and Lucy went to the front door.

'John's chauffeur is here,' she called out.

'We're leaving now,' he told Sir John.

Replacing the desk phone, he felt a twist of apprehension in his gut. What was he getting involved with again? There was always a danger, and he had Lucy to look after.

***

Edward and Lucy arrived at a detached Georgian house in Mayfair, and a grey-haired butler in a dark suit and red tie greeted them with a big, friendly smile.

'Sir John is waiting for you,' he said with a soft Irish accent. He then showed them into a spacious lounge with a black marble fireplace, red leather armchairs and Chesterfield settees. Two men and a woman stood by some open bi-fold doors that looked out onto a private courtyard.

'Mr Caster.' A middle-aged man in a green tweed suit and a paisley cravat approached them. He had a pale complexion, a broad brow and thinning dark hair. 'I'm John Henderson.'

They shook hands.

'I'm Edward, and this is my assistant, Lucy.'

Sir John nodded to her. 'We talked on the phone.' Then, he motioned to the others. 'This lady is Audrey, my wife.' She made a little nod with a tight smile. 'And this is Inspector Bradley from the Met.'

'How do you know about the abduction?' Bradley asked. The man was stern-looking, with dark eyes and bushy brows. He wore casual clothes and brown shoes.

Edward sensed his hostility. 'I received a psychic call from her, and she asked me to contact her father.'

'I know you're a celebrity psychic, and I've seen a couple of your shows on the telly.' He scowled. 'Not had much use for you guys. So where is she, and who abducted her?'

'I haven't made contact with her again.' He faced Audrey and John. 'She said they drugged her.'

Audrey gasped and held John's arm.

'At the moment, I believe she is all right.' Edward looked at Bradley. 'What happened?'

'Two days ago, Sophia went missing after a concert at the Albert Hall. Her friends reported that she had met a guy she knew in the bar and went off with him. The next day, Sir John received a call from the man who abducted her. He calls himself the Governor. He played a voice message from Sophia, pleading with her father to help her. Then, he demanded a ransom of five million pounds and insisted on no police involvement, or they would never see her again.'

'Bradley is not here officially,' Sir John said. 'But he's a friend and works at Scotland Yard.'

'Can you contact her again?' Audrey asked Edward.

'I can try. It would help to hold something personal of hers.'

'I'll take you to her room,' Audrey said, motioning for him to follow.

On the way, she glanced at him with a half-smile. She was still an attractive woman with curly chestnut hair and a slim physique. She wore a tight-fitting navy designer dress with gold bangles on her wrists. Only the fine lines on her face and neck showed her age.

'How old is Sophia?' he asked.

'Nineteen.'

'Any boyfriends?'

'She's had a few, but no one recently.' Audrey opened the bedroom door, and they entered.

The bedroom was expensively furnished with mirrored, built-in wardrobes, a king-size bed and a cluttered dressing table. A faint scent itched in his nose, and he sneezed. Audrey opened one of the windows, letting in a cool breeze. He stopped and closed his eyes briefly to sense Sophia's lingering presence in some things. On the bedside table was a red diary.

He sat on the bed and placed his left hand on the diary. Closing his eyes, he created the alignment to open his psychic awareness, then focused on linking with Sophia. After twenty minutes of calling her name, her agitated thoughts connected with him, and he experienced her fear and desperation.

'*Edward, thank God. I'm locked down here in the dark. I'm terrified, and they'll be back soon.*'

'*How many are there?*'

'*Two, maybe three men and a woman.*'

'*What happened?*'

'*I had a spiked drink and ended up here. I don't know where it is, but I did hear the men moaning about living in an old property. And it's a long way from London, maybe near the coast. When we arrived, I heard seagulls.*'

'*Any idea who they are?*'

'*The guy who abducted me was Anthony Radcliffe. I think the woman is called Maggie, and one of the men has a Scottish accent. What's going to happen?*'

'*They've contacted your dad and want a ransom. He is arranging for the payment.*'

'*Fuck! The light just came on, they're here—*' The contact abruptly ended.

Edward shuddered and opened his eyes to close his psychic awareness. Standing, he faced Audrey and John. 'Sophia is okay but afraid.' He turned to Inspector Bradley. 'She thinks there may be three men and a woman. They're in an old property, and she's locked in an underground place.'

'We knew a team must be involved.' He frowned.

'Got a name,' Edward said. 'The guy who abducted her called himself Anthony Radcliffe.'

He grimaced. 'Anthony Radcliffe? I'll check on him at the Yard. What we need to know is where they are.'

'What about a projection?' Lucy suggested to Edward.

'Haven't done that for years.' He paused and looked at Sir John. 'What's the situation with the ransom?'

'I'll have the money by tomorrow evening. But we have no details on the transference other than the police must not be involved.'

'How will they know?' Lucy puckered. 'Unless they're watching this place or have someone in the police force.'

Bradley raised an eyebrow at her. 'We're taking precautions here and at the Yard. But this team is unknown to us. The only contact has been with one guy, who calls himself the Governor, and he uses a voice scrambler.'

Edward glanced at Lucy. She was very astute for her age with a psychic shining, but emotionally, she was still a teenager. And now it bothered him about getting involved.

***

The light flickered on, and the sound of a metal door opening caused Sophia to stand abruptly, filled with a biting fear of what might happen next. Who were these people? Her heart raced, and she held her breath, trembling in the damp, musty confinement. A masked man in dark overalls stepped inside. Shaking, she slowly backed away, her arms crossed defensively.

'It's all right,' the man said in a kind voice. 'We're not going to hurt you.'

'Please let me go,' she pleaded submissively.

'We can't do that until your dad pays up.'

'He will pay. I know he will. And stop drugging me. It's making me ill.' She sat on the cot bed with her head in her hands and started to cry.

A masked woman in a floral dress entered carrying a tray with a ready meal, a mug of milky coffee and a bottle of mineral water. She placed the tray on the table.

'Don't cry, honey,' she said with a slight American accent. 'This'll soon be over.'

'I just want to go home!' Sophia said, trembling.

'You will. Now, drink your coffee, and you'll feel much better.' The woman motioned to the tray.

'She doesn't want to be doped again,' the man said. 'It's making her ill.'

'You sure?' the woman asked him.

'Yeah, she ain't going anywhere.'

'Okay.' The woman took the coffee, went into the back of the bunker, and tipped it into a chemical toilet.

'And please leave the light on. I hate being in the dark.' She dried her eyes. 'You don't have to punish or drug me. I'll do what you tell me. I want to go home.'

'You will soon, honey,' the woman said, and then she and the man left.

Sophia stood numb after the encounter. So, she had been kidnapped for money. Who would do that? She sipped some of the mineral water but didn't feel like eating. Lying on the bed, she tried to relax. The smell and dust of the old mattress itched in her nose. She managed to doze for a while, then woke when the metal hatch door opened.

The masked woman entered, and Sophia got up.

'Not hungry?' the woman said, looking at the tray. 'Here.' She handed Sophia some magazines and a chocolate éclair. 'We are not bad people. You'll be home soon. And we'll leave the light on, okay?'

'Thanks,' Sophia said, catching a hint of the woman's perfume. She watched her leave through the hatch door and noticed a masked man outside. The door slammed shut, and she was alone. At least the woman seemed friendly. It was a little comfort.

She trembled on the bed, gazing at the drab, mildewed, damp walls. After soothing her throbbing forehead, she tried to compose herself. Flipping through the magazines, she nibbled on the éclair. Fortunately, they had left the light on.

Later, she tried to contact Edward but couldn't make a connection. She needed to be in a specific state of mind, and he had to be receptive. Lying on the bed, thoughts of her parents overwhelmed her, and she broke down in tears. She knew her mother would be beside herself with worry, and her father would do anything to bring her back safely. She prayed for them and herself. Then, she felt a pang of guilt. It had been a long time since she had last prayed.

***

Edward and Lucy sat in the study by the dark marble fireplace that was warming the room with a glowing log burner. Sir John and Bradley sat opposite while Audrey stood solemnly looking out at the courtyard, smoking a cigarette.

'Have you any leads?' Edward asked Bradley.

'We suspect this Governor might be an American. I'm unofficially looking into it.'

'I wonder why they picked Sophia?' Lucy asked.

'Good point,' Edward said. 'Could someone close to Sir John be involved?'

'We don't think so.' Bradley shook his head.

Edward rubbed his chin. 'Who is this, Governor?'

'We're not certain. Over the years, he has turned up in various places, using aliases and disguises.'

'When is he going to contact you again?' Edward asked.

'Midday tomorrow,' Sir John said. 'But the money won't be here till late afternoon, early evening.'

Edward narrowed his eyes. 'Do you hand over the money and get Sophia back, or do they get it and tell you where she is?'

'I don't know yet,' Sir John said, balling his fist.

'It will have to be an exchange,' Bradley said. 'It's the only way you can be sure to get Sophia.'

Audrey came over. 'If only we knew where Sophia is. Can you help us, Edward?'

'You could try remote viewing,' Lucy suggested. 'I'll be your monitor.'

'Remote viewing, what's that?' Audrey asked.

'It's a form of psychic probing,' Edward said. 'But it's been a while since I've used that technique.' He sighed, not wanting to get too involved, but recalling Sophia's desperate situation and afraid of what might happen to her, he decided to try.

'It may help if we do it in Sophia's room,' Lucy said, facing Audrey. 'I'll need a pen and notepad. And it could take about an hour.'

***

Edward made himself comfortable in the yellow armchair by Sophia's bed, and Lucy sat at the dressing table.

'When you're ready,' she said, pen in hand.

Edward prepared his mind and created a focal point like a psychic inner eye sensitive to impressions.

'Sophia... Sophia... Sophia...' He used her name as an energised command and waited while holding the intent for any impressions to appear. After several minutes, an image of a sandy beach formed. Zooming into the image, he said, 'I see waves...a coastline with fishing boats and tourists. Now I'm moving away, inland, following a river. There are housing estates.'

'Can you see any street names or landmarks?' Lucy asked.

'Whoa.' He paused to focus as the impression changed. 'I'm in a field. There are buildings and a barn. It might be an old farm. Looks like a rusted tractor in an overgrown paddock.' He paused again. 'I'm back on the beach. Kids are playing, and some are watching Punch and Judy. Damn! I lost it.' He opened his eyes and found Audrey and Bradley in the room. 'My feeling is Sophia is somewhere near a coastal resort.'

'Plenty of coasts around the UK,' Bradley said dismissively. 'And a lot of seaside resorts. A name would help.'

'These are just impressions,' Edward said, ignoring Bradley's attitude. 'She could be anywhere.' He checked Lucy's notes on his remote viewing and recalled a feeling in the impression that she was there. But he had no idea of its location.

***

Sophia felt restless and hated being confined in this smelly, damp, claustrophobic space. She had been through the magazines and decided to explore the bunker. There were only three small rooms. One had the hatch door, two metal cot beds, a small table and a wardrobe. Inside, she found an old coat, a woollen hat and a pair of men's shoes that had gathered a thick layer of dust. In the coat, she found an old petrol lighter, a tobacco pouch and a small notebook with a shopping list for some hardware items and fittings from a shop called Godfreys.

In the middle room were seats, a table and an old rusting propane cooker. Against one wall were two metal lockers. She was about to open them when a light breeze on her face made her look up at a narrow air vent to the surface. One locker had cooking utensils, cutlery, plates and mugs. The other locker had some tins of beans, corned beef and tomato soup with faded labels.

The last room had a basin, towels, and a chemical loo that stank. Next to the loo was a new plastic container of Jeyes fluid. Holding her breath, she poured some into the loo and left. As she was passing through the middle room, she stopped. From the surface vent, there was a sound like a generator and a gentle movement of air.

She examined the metal hatch door in the bedroom and tried to open it, but it didn't move.

Lying on one of the smelly, bug-infested beds, she curled up and pulled her thin evening dress around her body. Being in this hellhole was a living nightmare. If only she hadn't gone with Radcliffe, she wouldn't be here. It was just for a bit of fun and to annoy Claire. Thinking of her home and friends, she closed her eyes and cried until she was exhausted. Then, she tried to connect with Edward again, but was too upset.

***

Later that evening, the butler brought in a trolley with refreshments and a decanter of brandy.

Edward looked at his watch. 'It's getting late. I guess we'd better be going.'

Audrey shook her head. 'You can stay here. We have plenty of spare rooms and a guest wing.'

'Not tonight.' Edward looked at Lucy, and she nodded.

'I'll be leaving now.' Bradley stood. 'I've got some work at the Yard in the morning, but I'll be here before midday.'

Sir John rose. 'Thank you. I appreciate your support.' They shook hands, and the butler showed Bradley out.

'It's a shame you are not staying,' Sir John said, pouring a large brandy. 'You fancy a nip?'

'I'll settle for tea. I need to keep a clear head. Have you any questions before we leave?'

'Are you sure Sophia is all right?' Audrey asked. 'I have a terrible feeling of...of what they could do to her.'

'Bradley says if we pay the ransom, Sophia will be fine.' Sir John raised his hand. 'I don't like it, but we have no choice.'

'I think Sophia is safe because they want your money. And I will continue investigating. If I need to contact you, I'll call that number you gave me.'

'Good man. I'll have Henry drive you home.'

As they left, Edward couldn't get Sophia out of his mind and wondered if she would ever be free. He glanced at Lucy. If she had been kidnapped, he would do anything to get her safely back, anything.

Chapter Two

In the bathroom, Edward ran a hot, soapy bath. The scent of lavender mingled in the humid air, creating a cocoon of warmth. While soaking, he thought of Sophia and got the impression that she was terrified of what they could do to her. And she was living in fear with no one there to help. He groaned as a nagging urge to find her persisted. In the past, he had helped locate missing persons, but did he want to get involved in this abduction?

Entering his bedroom, he found Lucy in a pink nightdress sitting on his bed.

'I thought I'd stay with you tonight.' She patted the bed.

'What's on your mind?' he asked, sensing her hidden agenda.

'You could try a projection. I'll be here to support you.'

'I've not done that for years. I don't know if I can still leave my body.'

'You can do it. And I can tell if you're sleeping or detached.'

He smiled at her. 'Your psychic ability is developing nicely. And I'm lucky to have you as a daughter and a valuable assistant.'

'Come on, Dad, let's try. I feel Sophia needs our help.'

'Okay, but we'll probably both fall asleep.' He lay on his back and let his body become heavy and detached. Focusing his attention on his forehead, he imagined his inner astral body separating from his physical body. Suddenly, Lucy nudged him.

'You were drifting,' she whispered.

He almost fell asleep four times but was stopped by her touch to his face.

Continuing to imagine and feel his inner body separating, a surge of energy and a sensation of freedom flushed his inner being. Abruptly, he was hovering above the bed, aware of his body and Lucy below. Before he could focus, an astral wind thrust him out of the house, and he was gliding through a clear night sky over the city like a bird. He liked the sensation of flight and being in the astral world, but there were hazards in this emotionally intense realm.

Focusing his thoughts, he made the command to find Sophia, and his vision blurred for a few seconds, and abruptly, he appeared in a field near an old, rusty tractor. In the distance was a cluster of derelict buildings like ghosts from a forgotten past. He hovered over fallen trees and weed-infested gardens to investigate. The place looked abandoned, but as he approached, he saw several vehicles parked inside an open Dutch barn. In the main building, there was a light inside. Entering, he found two men in dark overalls and a woman in a floral dress sitting by an old inglenook fireplace, talking.

'He should be here,' one of the men said.

'He'll be back in time,' the woman said dismissively.

'What about the girl?' the other man asked with a hint of a Scottish accent. 'Should have kept her doped, less hassle.'

'Let her be,' the woman said. 'She may not be going home. The Governor has an old grudge with Henderson.'

Thinking of Sophia, Edward was drawn into a small cellar to an old, rusted metal door. Pushing against the door, his hand went through the metal. Then, passing through the closed door, he found a woman in a blue evening dress dozing on a bed. He sensed she was Sophia and moved near, wondering if he could communicate with her. But she suddenly sat up. The shock almost broke his projection. He felt disoriented and found himself outside, hovering above the old buildings and losing control. He tried desperately to maintain the projection but lost it. The last impression was of a crater on the other side of the river.

He sat up and gasped, covered in sweat. Lucy was staring at him with her mouth open.

'What happened?' she asked.

'I got out and found her, but not the location.' He lay back, recalling his impressions from the out-of-body experience. 'I saw some of her abductors. It doesn't feel good. And their boss, the Governor, may have a grudge against Sir John.'

'You should talk to John about it.'

'Will do. But that was a difficult projection, and I don't have the control anymore. That may have been a one-off.'

'But you did it!'

'With your help.' He paused, thinking about the encounter. 'Something doesn't feel right. I don't trust these abductors, and I think we must find her. I might try connecting with her again.' He yawned and rubbed his head.

'Okay.' She climbed off the bed, smiling. 'Now you've opened up your psychic ability. It's like getting my dad back.' She hugged him. 'I'm going to get some sleep. See you later.'

'Pleasant dreams.' He watched her leave and smiled.

Thinking of Sophia, he sat cross-legged on the bed in the lotus posture. First, he aligned his spine, then linked the centres to engage his psychic awareness. After a few minutes, he became silent and receptive, then called Sophia's name repeatedly for a long time.

'Edward!' she suddenly responded. *'I've been trying to reach you.'*

'I need to know where you are. Is there anything in the bunker that can help, an old newspaper or something?'

'I've looked. There's not much here. Wait...I did find a shopping list in a coat. It was for a place called Godfreys. Hardware stuff.'

'Godfreys.'

'Yeah, it looks decades old, though.' She paused, then said urgently, *'Someone's coming.'*

He opened his eyes and went to find Lucy. She was in bed but not asleep.

'What's up?' She yawned.

'I need to find out about a company called Godfreys in one of the coastal towns. It may be a lead.'

Lucy sat up in bed and took her laptop off her bedside table. 'Godfrey's right.'

'I think it's a hardware store. I'm going to get dressed.'

Twenty minutes later, she called him. 'There was a Godfrey's department store in Lowestoft. It closed in 2015. Got some subsidiaries and been around since 1930.'

'Lowestoft, that's near Yarmouth, isn't it?'

'Yeah. I got it on Google, and it's a big place. Famous for its sandy beaches, the Broads National Park and even a Punch and Judy tradition. Here.' She handed him the laptop.

'That might be the place, but where is she? During the projection, I saw overgrown fields with a cluster of derelict buildings, maybe an old manor house or farm. The underground bunker is in the cellar of the main building.'

'I'll see what I can find out from online estate agents and the land registry in that area.' She looked up from her laptop. 'Could you get me a strong black coffee, please?'

'Of course. I think we both need one.' He paused, feeling acutely vulnerable and concerned for Lucy. He frowned, recalling the image of his dead wife in the burning car. It was like a warning. 'I'll call Martin in case we need someone to watch our backs.'

'Martin, that SAS guy! This is getting serious, Dad!'

'It may come to nothing, but I want to be prepared. And I have to keep my lovely assistant safe.' He winked at her.

***

Martin's phone rang for a long time before he answered.

'Hiya, Edward. You got me out of bed. What's up?'

'Hi, Martin. You got anything on at the moment?'

'Nothing I can't drop for you. Why?'

'I'm working on an abduction case and could do with some muscle. It would mean staying here and mainly looking after Lucy.'

'I thought you'd quit that psychic stuff.'

'Yeah, but something turned up. Can you come over?'

'What now, tonight? Well, okay, I'll be there in about an hour.'

'Thanks, Martin. I'll make it worth your while.'

Edward sat at his desk in the study and aligned his chakras to open his psychic awareness. It felt good to have regained this ability. He closed his eyes and focused his mind. Thinking about Sophia, he used the remote viewing technique, focused on the rusted tractor in the field, and allowed any impressions to arise.

After ten long minutes, he spotted a flock of seagulls scavenging in a field by the road. Suddenly, they took flight as a blue Range Rover approached. The vehicle drove toward some old buildings and then parked. Two men stepped out. His view was abruptly interrupted as he tried to focus on them. He sat up, sensing that one of the men had a dark aura. He leaned back and rubbed his forehead, worried about who these potential abductors might be.

Lucy entered with her laptop. She was dressed in a black skirt and a loose red top. 'There are a dozen possible locations in and around Lowestoft. I've got some pictures and stuff if you want to see them.' She placed her open laptop on the desk, and he went through the properties and development sites. One site looked particularly interesting. He Googled a street view and smiled, seeing part of an old tractor in an overgrown field. And across the river was an old clay pit. He tensed and got a gut feeling that this could be the place.

The doorbell rang, and Lucy stiffened.

'That'll be Martin.' He went to the front door.

Outside, a muscular man in jeans and a green sweater stood smiling with a grey knapsack on the ground.

'Thanks for coming,' Edward said and motioned him to enter.

'You helped me over that court-martial business, and I said I'd always be here for you.' He picked up the knapsack and entered the hallway.

'Hi, Martin.' Lucy smiled with a little wave.

'Wow! You have grown up since I last saw you.' He chuckled with a raised eyebrow.

'Lucy is my assistant.'

'We have a room for you,' she said. 'What's in that bag?'

'Just luggage and some military hardware. Got more in my vehicle.'

She made a face, then motioned for him to follow.

'I'll see you in the study when you've settled,' Edward said and gave him a friendly pat on his back.

***

Edward liked Martin and motioned for him to sit. He was a tough-looking man in his early forties with tattoos on his neck and arms. He used to be a sergeant in the SAS until he was falsely accused of murdering an officer. Fortunately, Edward was able to contact the deceased officer and discover the identity of the real killer and a witness to the crime. After the witness came forward, Martin was cleared at the court-martial. However, due to his attitude, he was offered an honourable discharge with some compensation, which he accepted. Edward sighed, remembering it had happened four years ago when Glenda was still alive.

Martin yawned and said, 'Lucy told me about the kidnapping. How can I help?'

'I want you to look after Lucy, but don't let her know.' Edward sighed. 'And if we locate Sophia, we may have to deal with the kidnappers. The police aren't involved, and time is not on our side.'

Lucy entered with coffee and sandwiches. 'Since we're working through the night, I thought this would keep us going.'

'Good idea.' Martin helped himself to a snack.

'Did you check out those properties?' Lucy asked Edward.

'I have, and one looked promising. It's inland by a river, and there's an abandoned tractor near the entrance.'

'That's worth checking out.' She gave him a stern look.

'It's a three-hour drive, and I'm not sure—'

'You got Martin here, which means you think Sophia is there.' She touched his arm. 'What've we got to lose?'

'It might be a waste of time.' Edward shrugged. 'And if we leave now, we won't be there till early morning.' He frowned at her, concerned. 'I think you should stay here.'

'No way, Dad! I'm coming with you.' She made a sad face and stood defiantly. 'Please don't leave me here alone. And we have Martin with us.'

He sighed, sensing her determination, and relented.

'I'll drive,' Martin offered. 'We can use my vehicle.'

***

While Lucy slept most of the way curled up on the back seat, Edward sat in the front and tried to relax, but a biting tension in his gut irritated him. He tried to connect with Sophia several times, but she was unreceptive, and he felt a twinge of concern.

'Didn't expect to get a call from you tonight,' Martin said, glancing at him with a raised brow. 'Got a gut shot that this was serious.'

'Yeah, and I've got a bad feeling about this abduction, and with Lucy involved, I thought of you.'

'I owe you, Edward.' He chuckled. 'And I'm getting an adrenaline buzz. God, I miss the action and thrill of covert operations.'

'I guess you've been in some dangerous situations?'

'Yep, dozens, mostly black ops.' He raised his eyebrows and grinned. 'Got shot up a couple of times, but the buzz is bloody addictive.'

'So that's why you guys do it. The kick of living on the edge of death.' He glanced back at Lucy, who was still sleeping. 'I'm glad you're with us, Martin.'

'Be an idea to get breakfast in Lowestoft, then find this development site.'

'Fine. I have an address for your satnav, but the site's a bit off the beaten track. Lucy printed off a Google view of the place. We may have to park and walk.'

Lucy groaned and sat up, stretching her back and rolling her head.

'How long to get there?' she asked, rubbing her eyes.

'Not long,' Martin replied. 'We're stopping at McDonald's or KFC to get something to eat first.'

'Sounds good. I prefer KFC.' She squirmed on the seat and yawned.

***

Sophia tensed when she heard people outside. She cringed with panic and stood as the hatch door opened. Two masked men in dark clothes and a masked woman in a green dress entered. She backed away, intimidated by their imposing presence. What were they going to do with her?

'It's all right, honey,' the woman said. 'We just want you to give your dad another message.' She held up a small recording device.

One of the men handed her a notepad. 'Just read what's on there,' he told her.

She held the notepad, but couldn't stop her hand from shaking.

'Read it!' a Scotsman insisted, balling his fist aggressively at her.

She tensed, seeing he had a gun in a holster on his hip.

'Hi, Dad, it's Sophia. I'm okay, and I've not been harmed yet,' she spoke, trembling. 'Please pay the ransom, or they are going to start hurting me.' She paused with her mouth open, looking at the men in disbelief. The Scotsman nodded for her to continue. 'You are being watched, Dad. Do not contact the police, and do what they tell you. Pay them today, or you'll never see me again!' She gasped, then screamed when the Scotsman punched her in the face and gripped her neck, digging his fingers into a nerve centre. Sobbing, she cried, 'Please do what they want, Daddy. I'm afraid!'

The woman switched off the recorder and handed her a box of tissues. Then they left, bolting the door from the outside.

Sophia stopped crying and held her bruised face. Her lip and nose were bleeding, and moving her jaw caused sharp twinges of pain. Using the tissues, she nursed her face while the thought of being hurt again terrified her. A shocking realisation surfaced, and she gasped. She was trapped, and they could easily kill her. Even if the ransom was paid, they could leave her locked in here, and without food and water, it would mean a slow death. She was at her abductor's mercy.

She sagged despondently on the smelly bed, then stiffened as a rat appeared from under the other bed. She shouted, and it scurried away. Shocked, she curled up on the bed with her head in her hands. There was so much she wanted to do with her life, and she was still looking for that special person to love, but it could all end in this rancid underground hellhole.

***

Edward didn't feel hungry and just had a carton of black coffee. He couldn't shake off a nagging feeling of danger but tried not to let it show.

Leaving the KFC car park, Martin set the satnav and headed inland.

'We could only get an approximate location,' Lucy said, leaning forward. 'Once we get through Oulton Broad, we head for a side road that runs along and across the river. There are several development sites in that area and a village with amenities.'

'Let's get to that village and start our search from there,' Martin said.

'Good. I need time to connect with Sophia,' Edward said. 'She's not receptive at the moment. I hope they haven't drugged her again.'

'And you were going to call Sir John,' Lucy reminded him.

'I'll wait till after midday. The abductors should have called him by then. And we don't know if Sophia is here. Psychic impressions are not clear-cut, and this could be a wild goose chase.'

'What's the ransom?' Martin asked.

'Five million.'

'Wow! That's a lotta dosh.'

'Yeah. My only concern is making sure Sophia is safe.'

'You think they might kill her?' Lucy asked wide-eyed, with her hand to her mouth.

'I don't know. Maybe if they get the money, they'll let her go. We'll know more when they contact Sir John.'

While Lucy and Martin went shopping for supplies, Edward stayed in the vehicle and tried to connect with Sophia, but she was still unreceptive. However, using his psychic awareness, he could feel her despair and sense her presence some miles from the village.

Lucy and Martin returned with soft drinks, snacks, and a map of the local area.

She opened the map on the backseat and studied the layout.

'A woman in the post office only knew of one development with a Dutch barn and gave us directions,' Martin said. 'Apparently, it's been vacant for decades.'

'Got it.' Lucy showed them the map.

'If we park here, in the adjoining site,' Martin said. 'We can stay out of sight, and I'll do some recon. Got communicators and body cams in my gear, so we can keep in touch.'

'Let's go,' Edward said, picking up on Martin's excitement, but a sense of dread flushed his being as his psychic awareness warned they could be entering a hornet's nest. He glanced at Lucy and wished he hadn't brought her with them. What the hell was he getting into? Then, thinking of Sophia trapped, alone and in danger from her abductors, he knew he had to find and help her.

Chapter Three

While Martin sorted out his gear, Edward sat with Lucy in the vehicle.

'Do you think Sophia is there?' she asked, helping herself to a Kit Kat from the goodie bag.

He closed his eyes and scanned the area psychically. 'Yes, I think so, but I can't connect with her at the moment.'

'I feel a little uneasy now we're here.' She sighed, lowering her head.

'I think you should stay in the village at the Inn. You would be safe there.'

'No.' She tensed and shook her head. 'But I don't mind staying here while you and Martin check out the site.'

'I don't like leaving you alone. Maybe you should have stayed at home.'

'No way! I'll be all right, Dad.'

Martin opened the driver's door and smiled. He wore camouflage overalls, a hard ballistic vest and military gear. He handed Lucy a military tablet and switched it on.

'That's linked to my body cam and communicator.' He moved the cam-eye and tapped his collar microphone. 'Can you hear me?' He chuckled.

'I can hear you and see clearly.' Her face brightened as she adeptly used the device. 'This is cool. It's like my iPad.'

'Also, just in case, this is for you.' He handed her a small handgun and showed her the safety catch.

She took the gun and held her breath. As she examined the weapon, her hands trembled. 'I've never held a gun before. It's small, yet heavy. And gives me the creeps.'

'It holds five rounds,' Martin told her. 'Keep the safety on until you want to use it, and aim low because the gun will jerk upwards when you fire. Okay.'

'Maybe I should stay with you?' Edward frowned at Lucy.

'That's a good idea,' Martin said. 'Let me check the place out first.'

'You're the professional.'

Martin chuckled. 'Here.' He handed Edward a pistol. 'That is one bad boy, so don't use it unless you want to kill someone.'

'That's scary! I hope I don't have to use the damn thing.'

'It's best to be prepared.' He checked his weapon. 'I'll do a quick tour, then return.' He closed the door and headed through the trees to the next site.

Lucy put the gun on the seat and picked up the tablet. 'He's moving towards the Barn,' she said, showing him the video from Martin's body cam.

Edward put the pistol in his coat pocket and then used the microphone.

'Can you hear me?' he asked.

'Loud and clear,' Martin replied. 'All seems quiet, and there's no one about. I'm just about to see what's in the barn.'

On the tablet, they watched as Martin crept around to the front of the barn. Inside were several vehicles, and he focused the cam-eye on them. There was a blue Range Rover, an old red BMW, and a small white pickup truck.

'Someone's coming over,' Martin said, and the video blurred for a few seconds.

On the tablet, Edward watched a man take two Tesco shopping bags from the BMW and carry them over to the large, dilapidated manor house.

'He's gone inside,' Martin whispered. 'I'm going to check out the other outbuildings before the big house.'

'It looks deserted,' Lucy said, viewing the tablet.

After a few minutes, Edward noticed Martin approaching the manor house when a woman came outside and made a phone call. He moved along the side of the property and around to the back door, which was unlocked.

'Silent mode, guys. I'm going in.'

'We've lost video,' Lucy said with a frown.

'He may have switched it off for stealth mode. I'm sure he knows what he's doing.'

Twenty minutes later, the video came back on. He was returning.

'Took a while to get out of that place. Be with you soon,' Martin said.

They watched Martin's video feed as he moved around the other side of the old house and through a thick copse of trees to their concealed vehicle.

***

'He's here.' Edward reached over, unlocked and opened the driver's door.

Martin climbed in. 'Three guys and a woman. Some are armed, and two look military, probably ex-Seals from the States. The other guy is Scottish. He seems to be in charge. Didn't see much of the woman, and I couldn't get to the cellar. The men take turns guarding the entrance.'

'We are amazed you got in and out of the house undetected,' Lucy said.

He shrugged. 'They're only using a couple of rooms. Most of the house is derelict. I heard them talking about leaving, and they're waiting to be contacted. Shame I didn't take a stealth transmitter with me. I'll get one out of the boot.'

Edward checked his watch. 'I think I'll contact Sir John. Find out what's happening with the transference and update him.' He used his phone. 'Hi, John. Edward here. Have they called you?'

'Yes, a few minutes ago. They're threatening to kill Sophia if they don't get the money today,' John's voice shook. 'I heard her pleading with them to stop hurting her. That got to me, and I feel so fucking helpless!'

'What about the transference?'

'They want the payment up front before releasing her. I've got a number to call when the money arrives. Bradley thinks it's all right, but Audrey and I don't like it. They could take the money and still kill her.'

'Are the police involved?'

'No. They said I'm being watched. Have you any news?'

'I'm working on finding where they have Sophia. I've got some leads on a place in Suffolk near Lowestoft. Fingers crossed, and I'll keep you updated. One thing: I think this governor has a grudge against you. Do you know anyone you have upset in a big way and may want revenge?'

'Several people may have. I'll need to think about that.'

'Is Bradley there?'

'Yes, he's about to leave for the Yard. He'll be back later to help with the transference.'

'Okay. Hang in there. I'll be in touch.' He disconnected and frowned with a shake of his head.

'You didn't tell him we may have found Sophia,' Lucy said.

'Something doesn't feel right. It's just a hunch that the abductors may be aware of John and could even have tapped into his phone. Also, we don't know if Sophia is in the cellar of that house.' He looked at Martin. 'And they want the money before releasing Sophia. I don't like that.'

'Nor do I.' Martin picked up the tablet and viewed the recording from his body cam. 'You said the bunker is like an extension to the cellar, which could mean it's beyond the footprint of the house, and here is a modern air-conditioning unit with feeds going into the ground.' He paused the recording and showed them. 'And on that small pillar is a covered metal grid, maybe an air vent to the bunker?'

'Well spotted.' Edward smiled at him. 'That needs checking out, and I'll try to contact Sophia.'

'I'll take a spare radio cam and dangle it down that air vent.'

'I'll monitor you.' Lucy took the tablet, switched it on and adjusted the settings. 'Don't know about you guys, but I'm trembling, on the edge.'

Martin touched her hand. 'It's just adrenaline. You'll be all right.'

***

Edward reclined the seat and closed his eyes. After a few minutes, he became receptive and called Sophia several times. At first, she seemed too distraught, but as he persisted, she sensed him.

'*Edward, is that you?*'

'*It is. How are you?*' He sensed her fear.

'*Thank God. I'm terrified. They hurt me. I'm afraid of them, and they have guns!*' She sounded desperate, her fear palpable even through the psychic connection.

'*Sophia, is there a vent shaft in the bunker?*'

'*What? Oh, yes, in the middle room. Why?*'

'*I want you to go to that room and see if anything comes down the air vent.*'

'*Are you here?*'

'*Not sure, but I think so.*'

'*Please, God, I hope you are. I'm alone and terrified of them.*' She disconnected.

Edward opened his eyes to find Lucy beside him, using the tablet on her lap.

'Martin is almost there,' she said, then focused on the video.

'I got through to Sophia, and she's waiting.'

'I'm here,' Martin told them. 'Turn on the ancillary feed to this cam-eye. I'm lowering it now.'

'Nothing yet. It's too dark in the shaft,' Lucy muttered. 'Wait, got some light, but the cam-eye is swinging.'

'Okay, I'll hold it till it settles. Is there any sound?'

Lucy turned on the sound in the cam-eye, and the video gradually stabilised. A dishevelled woman in a blue evening dress looked up at the cam-eye.

'Is that you, Edward?' she asked almost in a whisper.

Breathing out a sigh of relief, Edward used the microphone on the tablet.

'Sophia, thank God, we've found you,' he said. 'We can't get you out now because armed guards are inside. Just stay calm, and don't let them know we're here. This is Lucy.'

'Hi, Sophia. I'm Edward's daughter. I'll stay on this communicator while Edward and Martin devise a strategy.'

'Thank you so much. I was going crazy—' She paused, then whispered, 'Someone is coming. I'll see them in the bedroom. Don't speak, or they'll hear you.'

Edward frowned, the cam-eye couldn't see in that room.

'I brought you a meal, honey,' a woman said. 'We're waiting for your dad to pay up, then you can go home.'

'Are you taking me back, or is Dad coming for me?'

'That depends on the Governor. He's running this operation.'

'Governor?'

'Don't ask questions,' a man told her. 'Eat your dinner and be ready to leave.'

'I'm not hungry.'

'Eat the fucking dinner!' the man shouted aggressively.

'I'll stay until she's finished it,' the woman said in a friendly tone.

'Fine, we've got to get the vehicles ready.' There followed the sound of a metal door closing.

'Just eat the meal, honey. You'll soon be home,' the woman insisted. Then there was silence, and Sophia didn't return to the cam-eye.

'Hey, guys,' Martin called in. 'Two of the men are taking stuff out to the vehicles in the barn. I'm going inside to set up a stealth transmitter.'

'Be careful,' Lucy said.

'Silent mode, guys. I'm switching the cam-eye off.'

Twenty minutes later, Martin returned to the vehicle.

'I managed to put the transmitter near their lounge area. You need this to listen in.' He took a receiver out of his bag and switched it on.

'That's done, Thomas,' a woman said. 'The girl's sleeping now, and the dope should keep her out for hours. Anything from Mark?'

'Yeah, 'bout an hour ago,' the Scotsman replied. 'Got another delay on the money, but wants us ready to move. And he's pissed off with Henderson. We may have to top the girl.'

'There's no need to kill her. We can leave her doped for them to find.'

'That's up to Mark. He's the Governor.'

'What do you think of Pirtsha, Mark's moonchild?' she asked.

'She is frigging weird. Just being near her gives me a hard-on.' A man chuckled. 'Is she really an alien life sucker?'

'I don't know. Mark said her mother was the demon Lilith. Why don't you jump in bed with her and find out?'

'No bloody way!' There was laughter from the others. 'Where you going when we get our cut?' the man asked.

'Barbados got a nice little place out there,' the woman said. 'And you?'

'Back to the States, Mark has another operation in Washington to set up. Then I'm having a long, well-earned holiday.'

'What about you, Thomas?'

'It's back to the Highlands for me. My cut from this caper will keep me afloat for years. And I'm getting a bit old for this type of work.'

'I need to call Mark, and we'd better get ready to leave,' the woman said.

Edward touched Lucy's arm. 'Can you monitor them?' Then to Martin, 'Is it possible to get Sophia out of there? I don't think we have much time.'

'It is, but it would need two of us. We have to deal with three armed men and a woman. This will be dangerous, Edward.'

'Hey, I'm getting the sound of vomiting from the bunker,' Lucy said.

They listened for a few minutes.

'You there, Edward?' Sophia spoke in a weak, quiet voice.

'I'm here,' Lucy spoke into the microphone.

'They drugged me. I pretended to sleep, then made myself sick. I feel terrible and ill.'

'Sophia, I want you to rest until the drug wears off. You are not alone.'

'I will, but please don't leave me.'

'We're here for you.'

Lucy listened and paled, then looked at Edward. 'Got this going on in the lounge.' She set it to play aloud.

'...that's what Mark said,' the woman insisted. 'They think we're in Lowestoft and could be on to us.'

'Karl, check the grounds, and see if anyone is out there,' Thomas said.

'How the fuck could they find us?' another man asked.

'They got a psychic working for them,' the woman said. 'The police aren't involved, and Mark's not that concerned. We'll be out of here in an hour or so.'

'A fucking psychic! Is the Governor shitting on us?' Thomas chuckled.

'He's waiting for the money. Better get ready to leave,' the woman told them.

'Once we have the money, the girl don't matter,' Thomas said.

Martin faced Edward. 'How could they know about us?'

'I mentioned it to Sir John. Maybe they're watching him. And he had Bradley there.'

'Bradley's a policeman, right?' Lucy said. 'So, if they are watching, they would know Sir John has the police there!'

'Well intuited.' Edward smiled at his daughter and faced Martin. 'They're about to leave, and we don't have time to involve and convince the local police. We need to get Sophia out of there now.'

'Right, I'll need to get you some gear from the boot.'

'I'm just afraid,' Lucy said with a creased brow and touched the gun on the seat with her fingertips. 'Maybe I'm picking up on Sophia's fear of being locked in that underground place.'

Edward hugged her. 'You've connected with Sophia, and you're both developing psychic awareness.' Then he looked at Martin. 'I'm ready. Let's get geared up.'

'They will be looking for us,' Edward cautioned.

Chapter Four

On the military tablet, Edward watched Martin's body cam as he entered the Dutch barn.

'They're talking again,' Lucy said, turning the sound up.

'Well, Karl?' the woman asked.

'Couldn't find anyone in or near the outbuildings. They may not have found out where we are.'

'We'll be gone soon,' Thomas said. 'But stay on alert. And we'll take turns patrolling outside.'

'You guys can do that,' the woman said. 'I've got to finish packing our gear and clearing the place of our presence.'

'What about the girl?' Thomas asked.

'She'll be sleeping for hours.'

'Good. Hey, Mike, look outside and call the Governor for an update. He should've got the money by now.'

'It's gone quiet,' Lucy said, turning the sound down.

Edward picked up the microphone. 'How you doing?' he asked Martin.

'Got the charges set. But one of the guys has come out. Looks like he's calling someone on his phone. Now, he's heading for the outbuildings. Silent mode, guys.'

Edward watched Martin's body cam video on the tablet. He moved in the shadow of an old wooden structure, paused for a few minutes, then pounced on a young man as he came out of the barn and rendered him unconscious with a blow to the back of his neck.

Ten minutes later, Martin appeared and opened the driver's door.

'That's one,' Martin said. 'I've tied and gagged him in one of the barns.'

'I'm ready and geared up,' Edward said.

'Please be careful, Dad.' Lucy hugged and kissed him.

'Lock all the doors and keep the gun I gave you ready,' Martin told her.

Lucy picked up the gun, and Edward noticed her hand was shaking.

'Will you be all right?' he asked. For an intense moment, he felt a biting concern for her and didn't want to leave her alone.

As if picking up on his feelings, she said, 'You gotta do it, Dad. Get Sophia out, and don't get hurt.'

***

While Martin took point, Edward followed close behind and tried to stay out of sight. They went behind the house to the back door. The dim interior revealed bare, neglected rooms with peeling wallpaper. The place had been abandoned decades ago and smelled damp.

'I'll show you where to hide, then get ready to head for the cellar,' Martin whispered. 'If you encounter anyone, use the taser, not the pistol. And don't hesitate, or they will kill you!'

Edward took the plastic taser gun from its holster, and his hand was sweating. He shuddered with a chill in his gut. What the hell was he doing? There were armed men in there. His instinct was to get out of there fast, but he couldn't back out now. Gritting his teeth, he tried to ignore his fear.

Martin nudged him. 'Just keep focused!' He took out a remote detonator. 'Cover your ears. Here goes!'

Suddenly, three explosions thundered, blowing in windows and shaking the building.

'What the fuck was that?' the Scotsman shouted, and the men ran outside.

'Now!' Martin said, and they entered the lounge.

The woman gasped and was about to call out when Edward fired his taser at her. She cried out, shook violently, sank to her knees and passed out.

'Nice one,' Martin said. 'Now get the girl.'

As Edward turned to head for the cellar, a man entered from outside.

'Some fucker's blown up our vehicles—' He stopped as Martin's taser hit him. The man shuddered violently and then passed out.

An older man appeared at the door for a moment, then disappeared.

'Fuck!' Martin spat. 'Got a loose one. You get the girl. I've got to find that guy.' He adeptly used plastic ties on the man and the woman. Pausing, he listened, gave Edward the thumbs up, and left for the back door.

Edward cautiously descended the creaky wooden stairs that led to the small, musty-smelling cellar. His heart raced as he found the hatch door he had seen in his out-of-body projection. Touching the cold metal, his hand trembled. After a deep breath, he unbolted and opened the door to find a damp, dimly lit room. The air was thick with the smell of mould and decay. The only sound was the faint whirring of a generator somewhere. As his eyes adjusted to the dim light, he saw a cot bed in the corner of the room and a young, dishevelled woman in a crumpled blue evening dress. She was on the bed, cowering in fear and staring at him wide-eyed with her mouth slightly open.

'Sophia?' he asked, shocked by her appearance yet pleased to see her alive. 'I'm Edward.'

'Thank you, God!' She went and clung to him with sobs. 'I heard explosions.'

'We blew up their vehicles to distract them.'

'You all right?' Lucy asked through his communicator.

'Yeah. One of the men got away, and Martin went after him. He told me to get Sophia. We're on our way back to you now.'

'Please be careful. I love you, Dad.'

'I love you too.'

With the pistol in one hand and Sophia clinging to his arm, they made their way through the cellar and up into the lounge. The woman was still unconscious on the floor with her hands and legs tied, and she was gagged. The man was awake, but he was also securely bound and gagged.

'There's my bag and shawl,' she said, broke away and picked them up from an old wall unit.

'Come on.' He took her arm. 'We've got to get out of here.'

Leaving cautiously through the back door, he headed towards the barn, which was ablaze with fire and billowing smoke, and then out towards Martin's vehicle.

Gunshots sounded nearby. 'Shit!' He tried to contact Martin but couldn't get through. He sagged with a heavy sigh. The thought of Martin being shot chilled him. Was he on his own now?

'Dad,' Lucy's voice came through his communicator. 'Martin's not responding, and his video's blank. What's happened?'

'I don't know. I'll be with you soon.'

As he moved between the trees with Sophia, a man suddenly appeared, pointing a handgun at him.

'Drop the gun!' he shouted in a harsh Scottish accent.

Edward froze, holding his breath. Seeing the gun's muzzle in his face and the man's finger twitching on the trigger, he exhaled, and his body sagged. With no option, he dropped his gun.

Sophia clung to his arm. She was staring at the man and trembling.

'Who the fucking hell are you?' The man gritted his teeth, glaring at him.

'I'm just here to help a lady,' Edward said, trying to sound calm. But his heart was pounding, there was a chill of death in his gut, and he'd broken out in a sweat.

'You're one interfering son-of-a-bitch. I just shot your friend, and now it's your fucking—'

A gunshot shook the air. The man gasped and staggered, dropping the gun. A second bullet impacted his shoulder, and he fell, clutching his wounds. Lucy stood, pointing the gun at the man on the ground, her hand was steady, and the gun was cocked.

'Don't fucking move!' she yelled, aiming the gun at his head.

'Hi...guys,' Martin called in a strained voice. He appeared through the trees, holding his chest. He staggered over to the man on the ground, kicked him in the head and shot him in both legs. 'Payback time. Now, let's get out of here.' He pulled off his ballistic vest and showed Edward that it had stopped two bullets and damaged his body cam. Then he picked up the guns and took the man's phone from his pocket. 'Can't have you calling for help.' He kicked him again, threw the man's gun in the ditch, and headed for his vehicle. 'You'd better drive,' he said weakly to Edward, handing him the keys.

Lucy gave Martin her gun and took Sophia's arm. 'How are you?'

Sophia looked dazed and hugged Lucy. 'I thought we were going to die,' she said in a shaky voice. 'But, thank God, you saved us.'

A tremor of relief flushed Edward's nervous system. If it hadn't been for Lucy, he would be dead. He climbed into the driver's seat, and the others got in the back.

Looking around, he saw flames and smoke from the burning buildings and decided to leave. Driving towards Lowestoft, they saw a police car and a fire engine, probably going to the site. On their way to London, Edward began to relax the tension in his body, but his hands were trembling, and his head was still buzzing with adrenaline.

'Can you call Sir John and tell him Sophia is safe and coming home?' he asked Lucy and handed her his phone.

She made the call. 'I've set the speaker so you can hear.'

'Hi, John. We have Sophia. She is safe, and we're on our way to you.'

'I don't believe it. You actually have Sophia?'

She handed the phone to his daughter.

'Daddy, it's me. Thank you for sending these wonderful people.' She started crying, and Lucy hugged her. 'I'm all right. It's just the shock of it all coming out. I thought they were going to kill me.'

'Thank God you are coming home. Your mother is going to be thrilled. Now I have to make a call. We'll see you soon, darling.' She handed the phone back to Lucy.

'John, after Edward called you about us finding Sophia, someone tipped off the abductors that we were there. Someone from your end.'

'I only told Audrey and Bradley. They may have mentioned it to others. I'll look into that. Now, I must let Audrey know the wonderful news.' He disconnected.

Martin moved and groaned plaintively, holding his chest.

'Are you hurt?' Lucy asked.

'The ballistic vest stops the bullets from penetrating, but the impacts have bruised my rib cage. Damn, the guy was waiting for me like a pro, then went for you. Took me a while to follow.' He groaned again, then made a little smile at her. 'You, young lady, saved your dad's life. Well done.'

'I don't know what came over me. I saw him on Dad's cam feed and acted spontaneously.' She paused, then touched Edward. 'I just remembered, when I shot that guy, I sensed Mum with me.'

Edward smiled. He could sense Glenda with them in spirit, and his heart ached.

Chapter Five

Mark finished his martini and tried to relax. He was sitting at the desk in the study, waiting for the call to pick up the ransom, when when an emotional chill made him gasp—had something gone wrong with the operation? He called Thomas, but his phone was switched off. Then he called Maggie, Karl and Mike, but no one answered. Sitting back, he closed his eyes, took several deep breaths, and focused on remote viewing the site. After several minutes, he received vague impressions of buildings on fire. In the house, he sensed the bunker was empty and that the Henderson girl may have gone.

He stiffened and stood with gnawing anger burning in his mind. Smacking his forehead, he grunted, gritting his teeth. He didn't think they could find the Henderson girl. Maybe he should have been more concerned about Caster's involvement.

'What's up?' Pirtsha asked.

He frowned, instinctively aware of the alien spirit that glinted in her dark, unblinking eyes.

'I think the girl's gone,' he said, balling his fist. 'And I can't get through to Thomas or the others.' He paused thoughtfully, tried to calm his anger, and then muttered, 'Could that psychic be involved?'

She backed away from him. 'Are you sure about the girl?' she asked, crossing her arms over her loose blue smock.

He shrugged. 'Uncertain. However, I knew that psychic was helping Henderson, but I never thought he'd find the girl.' He sighed. 'Maybe I'm wrong.'

The desk phone rang. Pirtsha picked up the receiver, listened, and handed it to him. 'It's that policeman.'

'Mark,' Bradley said. 'We've got a major problem at the site. There have been explosions, the fire brigade and the police are there. And the girl has gone. Also, I checked with my contact at the bank, and Sir John has cancelled the delivery of the money.'

'I don't fucking believe it!' he yelled, stamping his foot.

'I'm still waiting for the details. But I heard someone's been shot. I don't know who yet.' He paused. 'Maybe that psychic found her. He was astute and even sussed she could be near the coast in Lowestoft.'

'How can one guy screw up my operation? He must have had help, and I've lost five million!'

'I'll find out more and get back to you.' He disconnected.

Mark punched the air. 'Two fucking months wasted setting this up. And to stop the payment, Henderson must have his daughter back. I will make him suffer for this and for what he did to my brother. I'll have Thomas kill his wife and daughter.'

Pirtsha paled with a tight frown, shook her head, and briskly left the room.

***

Sir John and Audrey had a long, emotional reunion with their daughter. There were many hugs and tears before they greeted Edward, Lucy, and Martin. Sir John took them into the study and paged his butler to bring refreshments.

Edward smiled with a sense of achievement at seeing Sophia back with her parents. He sat back in the comfortable armchair, drained from the ordeal, and closed his eyes. Briefly, he mentally saw Glenda, his late wife, smiling at him. He could tell she was very pleased they were safe.

'I don't know how to thank you.' Sir John wiped his brow with a tissue. 'We never thought we would see Sophia again. They threatened to kill her if I didn't pay. How did you find and free her?'

Martin chuckled. 'I guess you'll see it on the news. We made a hell of a mess and left them incapacitated.'

'After you called, I stopped the payment. It was still delayed, so I paid the costs and cancelled the delivery.'

'Where's Bradley?' Lucy asked him.

'At the Yard, working on another case, I think.' He frowned. 'But I'm not sure about him.'

'What security do you have here?' Edward asked.

'My butler and chauffeur-handyman live here. Why?'

'The guy who abducted Sophia is still out there. And he didn't get his five million. He might want revenge, and I think he has an old grudge against you.'

'Now Sophia is back, I could ask Bradley for police protection,' Sir John said.

'I don't trust Bradley.' Lucy creased her brow. 'Someone informed the abductors that we were helping you.'

'Hmm.' Sir John rubbed his chin. 'I'm still looking into that.'

'And I'm not sure about involving the police,' Edward said. 'It would mean telling them how we got Sophia out, and one guy got shot.'

'Shot!' Audrey gasped, wide-eyed.

'Yeah, it got messy as we were getting away.'

'And it's better to have your own protection,' Martin said. 'I know some ex-military who work in security. They are solid and can be trusted. But they will cost.'

'I've just saved five million. I can afford to hire the best.'

'You want me to call them?'

'Please do.' He glanced at Audrey. 'At least we won't have to sell our yacht,'

'You have a yacht?' Lucy asked.

'Yes, and two islands in the Caribbean. We usually spend winter there.'

'I'm still bothered by this Governor.' Edward turned to Lucy. 'Can you use the Internet and investigate the guy?'

'Sure, when we get home.'

'I've been thinking about some of my unsavoury associates,' Sir John said. 'And one does stick out. He was an investor who turned out to be an arms dealer, and I testified against him. His name is Brian Kempt.'

'Can you look him up as well?' he asked Lucy.

'I need to get cleaned up,' Sophia said, leaving with her mother.

***

Sophia climbed out of the scented bath and breathed in the warm, comforting steam. Was she really at home? She had desperately prayed for this, and now it felt like a dream, and she was afraid of waking up in that room.

'You're safe now,' Audrey said, and she helped dry her with a fluffy towel.

'It's so lovely to feel clean again and wash my hair. I've never felt so grubby and scared in all my life. And they hurt me.'

'It must have been terrible in that underground place.'

'It was a nightmare. I was alone in that smelly, vermin-infested cell, and I thought they were going to kill me or leave me in there to die.' She paused to calm her agitation. 'But I remembered Edward's TV shows and tried to contact him mentally. I had almost given up when he came through, and I asked him to contact Daddy.'

Audrey smiled. 'We used to like his shows, and you have always had that second-sight thing.'

'Without him, Martin and Lucy, I would still be there.' She pulled on a dress, sat at her dressing table and let her mother dry and brush her hair.

'I like Lucy. She shot one of the abductors who was going to shoot her father and probably me.'

'Whoa! Did she kill him?'

'No, she shot him in the arm, and he dropped the gun.' She looked up at her mother. 'Lucy saved her dad's life. I was there, and I like her and Edward. And Martin, of course.'

'I also like Edward. He has a presence that makes me feel comfortable and safe.'

'Mum.' She touched her with a trembling hand. 'It's so wonderful to be home and free.' Thinking of her ordeal sent a shiver through her body, and she started to cry. 'Sorry, I'm still haunted by what happened to me. I thought they were going to kill me or leave me to die in that hellhole.'

Audrey hugged her. 'Let's do your makeup. It might make you feel better.'

Sophia agreed and enjoyed her mother's presence and loving attention. She dried her eyes with a tissue and looked at her swollen, bruised face in the mirror. Cringing, she recalled the pain and impact of being punched. 'Why did they pick on me?'

A light tapping on the door made them look up.

'Come in,' Audrey said.

The butler appeared. 'Excuse me, madam. Sir John and the others would like you to join them at your convenience.'

'Thank you, Michael. Tell them we'll be down shortly.'

Sophia applied some makeup to her bruised face. Seeing her mother in the mirror behind her, she forced a smile, trying to ignore the horror of being abducted.

'Let's join the others,' Audrey said and hugged her. 'You're home now.'

***

'I can sense him out there, filled with anger and hate,' Edward said, then opened his eyes. 'I believe he is still a serious threat.'

'Who is?' Audrey asked as she and Sophia entered the study.

He looked up, surprised to see a very attractive Sophia, smartly dressed in a blue outfit and made up to cover the bruise on her swollen face. 'The Governor, the man who set up Sophia's abduction.'

'I may have met him,' Sophia said.

'When?' Edward asked.

'I think he might be Anthony Radcliffe. I never saw or heard him where they kept me. They wore masks and overalls, but I would have recognised him. He had a strong magnetic presence that got to me.'

'Do you have a laptop I can use?' Lucy asked Sir John.

'Use the one on my desk.'

'Can I join you?' Sophia asked.

Lucy agreed, and they sat at the desk with the laptop.

'What do you know about Brian Kempt?' Edward asked Sir John.

'It was a decade back. I invested in his company, only to find he was supplying arms to Afghanistan and other terrorists.'

'Hey, guys,' Lucy looked up from the laptop. 'I think we're on the news, BBC and Sky.'

Audrey picked up a remote and switched on the television on the wall above the fireplace. After flicking through the channels, she settled on Sky News. A female presenter was discussing a mysterious fire incident in Lowestoft. Then she handed over to their reporter at the site.

A young man holding a microphone frowned at the camera. 'The fire brigade says three vehicles were on fire, which spread to the barn and other buildings.'

The video showed the fire and the firefighters working to put it out. Then it panned to an ambulance, where a stretcher was loaded.

'One man was found shot in the arm, shoulder and both legs. He is alive and is being taken to A&E. And over here.' The camera panned to three police cars, where two men and a woman were being questioned. 'These guys and the woman were found with their wrists and legs tied with plastic straps. What happened here is still a mystery. At the moment, no one is saying anything. Back to you in the studio, Nancy.'

Audrey turned the sound off and faced Edward with her hands on her hips. 'What happened?'

'We started the fire to get them out of the house. While I went to get Sophia, Martin overpowered and tied up three of them, but the fourth guy shot him, and that guy was about to kill me when Lucy shot him in the arm.' He looked at his daughter with deep admiration.

'You were shot!' Audrey said to Martin and put her hand to her mouth.

'Luckily, I was wearing a hard ballistic vest.' Martin stood and opened his shirt to show them two large, dark bruises on his chest. 'Because of that, I shot him in both legs.'

'That guy hurt me,' Sophia said with an edge in her voice. 'I would have killed them all!'

'There was no need. We got you out without killing anyone,' Edward said, smiling at her.

The doorbell rang. After a few minutes, the butler entered with two men and a woman dressed in dark, casual clothes.

'Good to see you,' Martin greeted them, then faced Sir John. 'This is Vincent, Alex and Craig. They are ex-Special Forces and highly trained. I suggest you choose one of them as a personal minder for Sophia and have the other two guard yourselves and the property.'

Edward viewed them. Vincent was a slender yet muscular man with short black hair, brown eyes and a hawk-like brow. Alex, the female, was a muscular woman with fair hair and tattoos on her neck and hands. Craig looked like a jockey with a compact body, a shaved head and tattoos on his neck. They were all in their late twenties.

'Can I choose?' Sophia asked and picked Alex.

'Are you armed?' Audrey asked them.

'We are, madam,' Vincent said, opening his jacket to show her his shoulder holster and handgun. 'And we work as a team.' He motioned to the ear communicators that they all wore.

'Well, I feel better that you're here. What do you think, John?'

'Fine by me. My butler will arrange payment for your time, and you can stay in the guest wing.'

'Thank you, Sir John,' Alex said, smiling at Sophia. 'We would like to check out the security of your house and grounds, then report back to you, sir.'

When they left with the butler to show them the property, Sophia asked Martin, 'Was Alex in the Special Forces?'

'Sure was. I also worked with her on several operations. She is one of the best, dependable, loyal and deadly. You have an excellent minder.'

'Er...guys,' Lucy said with a deep frown. 'Brian Kempt did three years in prison, then left for South America and disappeared.'

Sophia went over and viewed his photo on the laptop. 'That's not Radcliffe, but he looks like the guy who drove Radcliffe's Range Rover.'

'As for the Governor, I found some references to a Mark Skully. An investment banker in New York. Allegedly, he ran a scam that ripped off many wealthy people before disappearing. I have his picture from the time of the scam. It was taken in Las Vegas some years ago.'

'That's him!' Sophia scowled. 'He's a bit older now, changed his appearance, but that's the man who abducted me.'

Edward looked at his watch, then glanced at Lucy. 'Time to go?'

'No!' Audrey shook her head. 'Please stay with us. We have enough spare rooms. You too, Martin.'

'I would like that,' Sophia said, looking at her father.

'Might be a good idea.' Martin nodded. 'While this Skully is out there, I think it would be safer to stay together.'

Edward agreed. He had ignored the danger from the terrorists, and Glenda had died. Now, he was concerned about Lucy.

'Better to be safe than sorry,' Audrey said.

'I don't mind.' Lucy made a little shrug, giving Edward a look of approval.

'Okay,' Edward said. 'I can sense him out there, and he's not alone. I could try remote viewing to locate them.'

'Can I get some clothes and stuff from home?' Lucy asked.

'Only if I come with you,' Martin said, then to the others, 'You'll be safe with my team here.'

'Don't be long,' Edward said.

'I'll pick up some of your stuff too.' She hugged him and left with Martin.

Alex entered. 'You got some security problems.'

'Can you fix them?' Audrey asked.

'Of course, it's why we're here. We'll also be installing CCTV cameras inside and outside the building. Your butler said we can use the cloakroom to set up our monitoring equipment.'

'That sounds ideal,' Audrey said.

Edward stood and stretched his back. 'I need to lie down for a while.'

'Come, I'll show you to your room.' Audrey motioned for him to follow.

On the way to the east wing, she said, 'Sophia and I loved watching your shows. You helped a lot of people. Why did you stop doing them?'

'Something happened, and it changed my life.' He didn't want to talk about his wife's death.

'Here's your room,' Audrey said. 'It has an adjoining room for your daughter.' She touched his arm. 'And I must thank you for finding and bringing Sophia back to us. I thought we had lost her.'

'You're welcome.' He smiled at her.

'I'll leave you to settle in. If you want anything, just buzz Michael, our butler. There's a pager on the bedside table.'

Once alone, Edward removed his jacket and dropped it on the chair by the bed. On the wall above the bed, he saw a painting by Mondrian with intersecting lines and planes of red, yellow and blue. He ran his fingertips over the surface of the canvas and realised it was an original work by the artist.

After stretching his aching limbs, he removed his shoes, lay on the double bed and closed his eyes. His body ached, and he was still trembling from the ordeal. Gradually, he drifted off to sleep. Briefly, he was out of his body at the site, viewing the smouldering remains of the vehicles and barn. Then, he was in the bunker and sensed someone was there, but couldn't see anyone. As he turned to leave, a hand gripped his shoulder. Instinctively, he pulled away and woke with a start to find a shadowy figure in the room that thrust a psychic spike at him before it dissipated, leaving a chill of something dark and unholy.

Chapter Six

PART TWO

Mark Skully came out of his trance state and shook himself. Pirtsha, Brian and Bradley were on the sofa in the lounge, watching him.

'I got to that psychic,' he told them. 'But he repulsed me. I'll need to use a power rite next time. Couldn't get much on what was going on there, and I sensed a lot of people in the house, maybe the ones who got the girl from us.'

'I'll visit Sir John and find out what's happening,' Bradley said.

'He might be on to you, but do it anyway.'

'I still can't believe they shot Thomas,' Brian said, pulling out a pack of cigarettes from his jacket and lighting one. 'He's the best hitman I've ever known.'

'And why shoot him in the arm and legs?' Pirtsha asked.

'That's a punishment hit,' Mark said. 'What about the others?'

'They're saying little and pleading ignorance,' Bradley said. 'They were the victims, but there are a lot of unanswered questions over some weapons and equipment.'

'Thomas is a big loss.' Mark sat back, thinking of Henderson. 'I need to hire another hitman.'

'I know someone,' Bradley said, taking out his phone. 'He's an oddball but good at stealth attacks. His name is Jonas.'

'I've heard of him.' Brian rubbed the stubble on his chin, then puffed on his cigarette. 'He's known as the Shadow and is utterly ruthless.'

'Good.' Mark smiled. He wanted Henderson to suffer.

***

Sophia was in her bedroom, getting dressed, when Alex knocked and entered. She smiled at her, feeling a warm glow inside. Alex had a muscular body with tattoos of birds, daggers and roses adorning her skin. Moving close, Sophia caught a whiff of Alex's subtle musk perfume and felt excited. She felt safe with Alex and sensed a mutual attraction, but didn't know if she could trust her psychic awareness.

'What was it like in the forces?' she asked, pulling on a long orange cardigan.

'Boring most of the time, sitting around for months, but the action made up for it.'

'Have you killed anyone? Sorry, I shouldn't ask.' She put her hand to her mouth.

Alex shrugged, making a face. 'I've been in the thick of it, and it's kill or be killed.' She sighed. 'Martin is one of the best, even though he got shot. We live with the fear, on the edge, and honestly, it's an addictive buzz.'

'Have you ever been shot?'

Alex pulled up her sweater and showed Sophia a jagged scar on her side. 'Got one there, another in my thigh and one in my arm. The ballistic vest stopped the other two.'

'What happened?'

'A guy shot me with a machine pistol. He would have finished me, but Martin broke his neck.'

Sophia looked at her with an open mouth. 'You live a strange kind of life, Alex. I never realised these things went on until I was abducted.' She shuddered, recalling the fear of being captive in that dark hellhole, and they hurt her. She bit her lower lip and started to cry.

Alex hugged her. 'You're still in shock. Just let the emotion come out. It will take some time to recover. And no one is going to hurt you while I'm here.' She tapped the gun in her shoulder holster.

Sophia felt comforted and sobbed, clinging to her until the emotion eventually passed.

'Thank you,' Sophia said, admiring Alex and enjoying her inner strength. She felt a strong urge to kiss her, but didn't know how Alex would react.

***

Edward smiled at Lucy when she brought a suitcase in and dropped it by his bed. She had changed her outfit and was wearing jeans with a blue sweater. He tilted his head and smiled. She was so like her mother that it made his heart ache.

'Got you a change of clothes and your shaving gear. We stopped at Martin's place to pick up some stuff. He's staying in the guest wing.'

'And you're next door.' He smiled at her affectionately.

'Feels strange being away from home.' She gave him an odd look. 'How are you, Dad?'

He shrugged, got up and hugged her.

'I sense you're worried.' She looked him in the eye.

'Yeah, this isn't over. And I feel him out there...waiting and scheming.'

'What's he like?'

'A dark soul. An occultist. That could be how he's never been caught.'

'An occultist? Is that like being a psychic?'

'They have psychic awareness but also use a form of ritual magic to influence people and situations. And he is aware of us here.'

Lucy pulled away. 'Now I'm worried. At least we're not alone. What are we going to do?'

He pulled on his jacket and shoes, then sat in the chair by the bed. 'Let's start with remote viewing.'

She sat on the bed and took a notepad and pen from her handbag. 'Okay, when you're ready.'

Edward closed his eyes, took several slow, deep breaths, and focused his inner eye to see the man behind Sophia's abduction.

At first, his vision was clouded for a long time. When it finally cleared, he saw a high-rise apartment building and was drawn to the penthouse. However, he couldn't enter or see inside. 'I can see the apartment, but I can't get in. There's a roof garden with a pergola and some furniture,' he said, pausing momentarily. 'Oh, I lost focus. I sensed several people in the penthouse, but the place is enveloped in a psychic mist.'

'Any idea where it was?'

'No. It could be in any city.' He rubbed his forehead and eyes.

'You want to try again?'

'No. I don't want to probe that man again today. He is already aware of me.'

Lucy made a little gasp. 'Has he connected with you?'

'As I woke, his presence was briefly in the room. My impression was of a dark, powerful soul.'

'That isn't good, Dad. What are we dealing with here, black magic?'

Edward sagged as memories surfaced of his first encounter with the occult world as a child. The impact of that experience profoundly changed his life.

***

Sophia noticed Bradley downstairs, talking to her father in the hallway by the open front door. She felt a chill and gripped Alex's arm. 'I don't trust him. And I don't want to see him.'

Alex used her communicator. 'Vincent, have a word with John and get rid of the policeman. He could be a security risk.'

'On it, Alex. I've already told Sir John to deny that the abduction happened. I'll go and back him up.'

After some heated words, Bradley left, and Vincent closed the front door.

Sophia went down to see her father. 'What did Bradley want?'

'He wanted you to make a statement about the abduction. But I told him there was no abduction. It never happened. You were staying with some friends and crashed out for a few days. The calls were just a joke. That should stop any more of his involvement. He was mad and shouted, but Vincent insisted he was not welcome, and he left.'

'Good. Lucy thinks Bradley could be involved with the abductors.'

'Really!' His eyebrows narrowed, and he clenched his fist. 'He also wanted to know what was happening here with these security people. I told him nothing. I guess I won't be seeing much of him now. And I might speak with some of my Masonic associates in the police force.' He put his arm around her shoulders, and she rested her head on his chest.

She made a happy sigh. It felt good to be home and safe in his arms.

***

Edward felt another uncomfortable pang in his gut. Sitting out in the garden with a cup of tea, he could sense Skully was up to something. Occasionally, he was aware of him scanning the place, probably using remote viewing. Twice, he had used a psychic spike to repulse Skully. Who the hell was this guy? He finished his tea and stood as Lucy came over.

'Here you are,' she said, then frowned at him. 'You got that look, Dad. What's up?'

'It's like the threat from those terrorists. We thought we were safe.'

'Dad! You weren't to blame.'

'I should have been more—'

'Please don't punish yourself. We need you. Sophia and the Hendersons need you.'

He hugged her, making a little sob. 'Your mother died because of me.'

'You couldn't have saved her.'

'I could, but I was afraid to use the knowledge.' He sighed heavily and lowered his head.

'What knowledge?' She shook him, looking wide-eyed. 'Tell me!'

He pushed her away. It was something he had never told her or anyone apart from Glenda, who made him promise never to use that dark knowledge. Now that Lucy was old enough to know the truth, and in their present situation, he decided to tell her. 'You don't understand. It involves the Night Side of Eden!'

'Night Side of Eden? That doesn't make sense, Dad.'

'Your mother called it the devil's art.' He took a deep breath and faced her. 'When I was a child, they said I was possessed. I wasn't, but I was different.' He turned away, recalling when he knew personal things about people and could influence them. His parents were afraid of him. At twelve, he was expelled from school for tormenting the teachers with curses. After that, he hid his psychic ability and tried to live a quiet, solitary life.

Lucy looked at him with her mouth open. She was shaking and stepped away from him. 'Dad, you're frightening me.'

He tried to smile. 'As a kid, they called me the devil's child. Your mother knew and made sure I never used that knowledge.'

'What is this knowledge? And why are you so afraid of using it?'

Seeing the desperate look in her eyes, he decided to tell her. 'Human ignorance and conditioning are bliss. The Night Side opens an altered state of being, and you lose your innocence. Eventually, you lose your human soul.'

Lucy gasped, stepping away from him. 'I can sense it in you now like a dark shadow.'

'I keep it in abeyance. If I don't use it, then I am free.'

'I see. Contact with this Skully is awakening your Night Side.'

'Your intuition is correct, and your psychic awareness is developing. Fortunately, you don't have that dark shadow on your lovely soul. Few people have your level of psychic ability.'

She made a face and sagged in tears. 'Oh, God!' She hugged him. 'Dad, this is crazy. What're we going to do?'

He tried to comfort her. 'It will be all right,' he whispered, feeling this was far from over.

***

In the study, Edward found Vincent and Sir John at his desk, viewing a military tablet and discussing security. When Vincent looked at him, Edward sensed their concern and went over.

'Someone has been snooping around here,' Sir John said.

'We've installed CCTV cams around and inside the property.' Vincent motioned to a man's face on the tablet. 'Caught this guy several times.'

'Who is he?'

'We don't know, but he was casing the place.' He paused. 'At the moment, Alex is minding Sophia, Craig is minding Audrey, and Martin is managing our surveillance monitors.'

Lucy entered and came over. 'Something doesn't feel right. Have you noticed the atmosphere?'

'We're being stalked,' Vincent said with a slight grin. 'There is always a sense of apprehension.'

'No, it's something else.' She creased her brow and pouted.

'I feel it,' Edward said, closed his eyes and psychically scanned the place. 'He's focusing on us.'

'Who is he?' Sir John asked.

'Skully, the man who abducted Sophia.'

'What can he do?'

'I'm not sure. I sense he's a powerful occultist and could try to influence some of us or even summon entities to harass and frighten us. More likely, he will send an assassin to get his revenge.'

'I understand an assassin, but summoning demons is a bit OTT,' Vincent said with a twisted smile.

Edward remained silent. He had encountered some of these entities as a child. They used to wait for him to sleep and take him away somewhere. He would wake in the morning with no recollection of where he had been. But the memory of those alien beings haunted his young mind.

Martin entered. 'I've got the Scotsman's phone.' He showed it to Vincent. 'Most of the data's been deleted. But the last call came after we left the site. It might be from the Governor. There's a short voice message.'

'Thomas, what the fuck is happening? Get back to me ASAP!'

'That could be Skully?' Lucy said. 'Can you trace the call?'

Vincent smiled at her and took the phone. 'I'll see what I can find out using Spyic.'

'Why does Skully want revenge?' Lucy asked.

'I don't remember anyone called Skully,' Sir John said. 'I suppose he could have used an alias.'

'If we can locate Skully?' Martin raised his brow. 'That would give us an edge.'

Edward agreed. 'I could try a psychic probe. Play the message again.'

'Thomas, what the fuck is happening? Get back to me ASAP!'

Edward focused on the voice and opened his inner eye. For a brief moment, he saw a man standing on a roof garden with a young woman and two men. In the distance, he noticed the top of a large stadium. It looked familiar. As he focused, the man's psychic shield abruptly repulsed him.

'Shit! I think he's Skully,' Edward said. 'And I sensed he's in London, possibly near a stadium like Wembley.'

'It's a burner phone,' Vincent said, looking up from his laptop. 'The number is not on any public records and has no personal data.'

'Figures,' Martin said. 'They're professionals and know how to stay anonymous.'

Chapter Seven

E dward called a meeting, and everyone assembled in the lounge. They included Michael, the butler, his wife, Susan, their cook, and Henry, the chauffeur.

'Now we have Sophia back and security people here,' Audrey said. 'They won't come for her again. We're safe.'

'I'm not so sure.' Edward shook his head. 'I feel the Governor, Skully, wants revenge for losing the money, and he has a grudge against Sir John.'

'What can he do?' Audrey asked.

'They're wicked!' Lucy said, contorting her face. 'They used a car bomb, and my Mum died!' Lucy choked, covering her eyes.

'I'm so sorry.' Audrey touched Lucy's arm. 'I didn't know. That must have been terrible for you.'

'It was the worst time in my life. And I miss her every day.' She wiped the tears from her face with her hand and sobbed. 'She burnt to death in the car. We couldn't help her. Then it was over and...'

Sophia came over and hugged Lucy affectionately, and Vincent held her hand.

'Sorry. It still gets to me.'

Edward sighed, masking his grief. They had seen Glenda die in the fire.

'We're dealing with people who abducted Sophia and could have killed her,' Martin said. 'I got shot up by a pro. These people are bloody dangerous, and like terrorists, they torture and kill people to get what they want, and they hate people who interfere.'

Sir John glanced nervously at Audrey, sighed, and asked Edward, 'What is your take on this situation?'

'At the moment, I think Skully is letting us relax and lower our guard. He is also trying to influence us to be careless. Watch your thoughts and help each other.'

'I've been getting urges to leave the house with Mum to go shopping. And thoughts of getting away from you guys,' Sophia said, motioning to Alex, Vincent and Craig.

'And I've been getting annoyed about having all these people here,' Audrey said. 'I've also been getting persistent urges to go shopping with Sophia and get away from the house. Yet we don't need anything.'

'They're using remote influencing. You must help each other to transcend these urges,' Edward told them. Then, he stood and faced Sir John. 'It was six weeks after the terrorists were convicted that someone rigged my car, and it killed my wife. I don't want that long-term threat to hang over your family. We need to stop Skully.'

'How?' Lucy asked and paled.

'I must find and confront him.' He paused thoughtfully. 'And I'll need a damn good strategy to deal with this occultist.'

'No!' Lucy said with a shake of her head, then sat silently with her head in her hands.

'I need you to maintain this level of security for a week or so,' Edward said. 'During that time, I will try to locate and deal with Skully. But I will need all of your support.'

'What do you want us to do?' Sir John asked.

'I want you to form a circle around me.' He looked at Michael, Susan, and Henry. 'How do you feel about joining us?'

'We have always felt part of the family, sir,' Michael said. 'And we enjoyed your TV shows.'

'I've only been with the family for a few years after my wife passed away,' Henry said. 'I am also a fan of yours and feel privileged to be here.'

'Okay, clear the floor and arrange the chairs in a circle.' He glanced at Lucy, who nodded her approval.

'Is this like a coven?' Audrey asked with a raised brow.

'Similar. We're creating a group energy that will help strengthen each of you and block Skully's remote influence. Also, I need to use the collective energy to aid my projection. Does anyone want to drop out?'

'We need someone to monitor the security systems,' Martin said.

'Can you monitor it remotely?'

'We can use a tablet. I'll get one.' Vincent left the room.

'Do you know what you're doing?' Lucy asked Edward.

'I failed your mother by ignoring the terrorist threat. Now, I will not fail.'

'Mum would be proud of you, Dad.' She looked up at Vincent when he returned. He winked at her, and she smiled warmly at him.

Edward used the bathroom and washed his face. Looking in the mirror, he froze, recalling his childhood experience of playing with the forces and potencies of Otherness. Part of him was terrified, while a deeper part wanted to explore that altered state of consciousness again. As a child, he recalled leaving his body and exploring the solar system. He viewed Mars, Jupiter, Saturn and Uranus, and, at the edge of the solar system, he experienced the vastness of Cosmic Space. Finally, he entered the Night Side of Eden, and its dark alien energy profoundly changed him. Now, he felt torn between encountering the exciting, mysterious realm of Otherness and the chilling fear of being lost or consumed in that vastness beyond physical space.

'Dad,' Lucy called him softly. 'They're ready.'

He gave her a knowing smile. 'I see you like Vincent.'

'Yep, he's an interesting guy.' She blushed. 'He's been telling me about his life. He joined the forces when his parents split up, and he didn't get on with his new stepdad. Anyway, it's nice to have him and the others here. Makes me feel safe.'

He hugged her but was unsure about her involvement with Vincent, who was probably ten years older than her. Still, it was good to see her happy again.

There was an eerie silence surrounding the group of people. The room was now dimly lit, and the antique furniture had been moved away so the group could form a circle. They sat on mahogany dining chairs, looking at Edward with curiosity and concern as he entered the circle. One by one, he touched and linked a psychic thread to each of them.

'First, we will bond the group and charge the circle.' He took several deep breaths and repeatedly intoned the sound Omm.

Lucy then sounded the Omm, and the others joined in.

'Close your eyes, and keep humming the Omm,' he told them. Then he sat cross-legged on the carpet in the lotus posture with his back straight. Aligning his spine and chakras, he focused his mind and intoned a psychic invocation to bond the group into a collective force. Gradually, the psychic energy built up within the circle.

Exhaling slowly, he focused on his crown centre outside and above the top of his head. As the centre opened, he rose out of his body. Hovering above the group, he thought of Skully's penthouse, and he abruptly appeared on the roof garden. No one was there. Cautiously, he entered the apartment and encountered fluctuating mists of disturbing energy that shielded the place psychically but not from his empowered astral projection.

In one room, he found a strange woman who radiated the alien aura of a moon-child. She glanced at him, and her eyes narrowed with intensity. Her probe washed through his being, and for a moment, he froze, confused by their strong connection. Then she frowned, switched off her laptop, stood and left. He followed, and she entered a study where a man sat in an armchair reading an old manuscript. He sensed this man could be Skully.

'Mark, someone's scanning us,' she told him.

'Who?' He stood balling his fist.

'I don't know. But he's here.' She motioned to Edward's presence in the hallway.

Mark suddenly pushed her aside and yelled a command that chilled and forced Edward's astral body out of the apartment. Desperately maintaining his projection, he glided down to the street below. After searching for his location, he ended the projection and returned to his body within the circle. He slumped, then stretched, rolled his head, and stood. Taking a deep breath, he composed himself and faced the group.

'You can stop the chanting now and open your eyes.'

'How did it go?' Lucy asked, getting up.

'I managed to get into his apartment. And I saw a small woman, quite an extra-ordinary creature like a moonchild.'

'Moonchild?' Lucy gave him a puzzled look.

'A female with an alien soul. I've known of them but never encountered one. Then, I think I saw Skully, but he repelled me with a psychic spike.' He looked around at the group. 'How did it go for you, guys?'

'I've never known such deep inner peace,' Sir John said.

'The humming was amazing.' Audrey beamed. 'I felt my stresses and concerns dissipate.'

'Me too.' Sophia nodded with a smile.

Alex went over to Edward and hugged him. 'Thank you. That session healed something in me from my childhood.'

'That was transcendental,' Vincent said, and Martin agreed.

Craig wiped a tear from his face and chuckled.

'Would anyone like some refreshments?' the butler asked. He was beaming.

Henry bowed to Edward and said, 'Thank you.'

'Did you locate them?' Martin asked.

Edward nodded. 'I got the name of the street, and I think it's a few miles from Wembley Stadium.' He gave Vincent the name.

Ten minutes later, Vincent called out from John's desk in the study.

'Got it! The penthouse is rented out to Mr Mark Chandler on a six-month lease. I've got the floor plan from Rightmove. It even has a roof garden. Nice place.'

Edward went over and viewed the apartment on the laptop. 'Is it possible to stake the place out?'

'I can send Craig?' Vincent said.

'No.' Martin shook his head. 'Better to use Harry. He's a private eye. I'll call and see if he's available.'

'Do you have a plan?' Sir John asked Edward.

'I'm working on several strategies, but I need to know how powerful he is. We'll do another group session after dinner to find out more.'

'I like the group sessions,' Audrey said, and the others agreed.

After a few minutes, Martin came over, putting his phone in his pocket. 'Harry has sent someone to stake out the penthouse.'

'Good.' Edward tensed and became psychically aware of Skully in the shadows. He was up to something.

***

Mark was smoking a cigarette with Brian and Bradley in the lounge when Pirtsha entered, carrying a tray with mugs of tea for them. He smiled at her. She was his surrogate child and the only successful creation of a moonchild that he knew of. Stubbing out his cigarette, he frowned at the memory of her conception, which had occurred during a magical ritual. While probing Otherness beyond physical space, the demon Lilith pulled him into that realm. There, she extracted some of his essence and created the female he would need to nurture and educate. Pirtsha's rapid development took several years. Now, he utilised her to open a safe portal to Otherness and to energise his rituals with the Dark Current. However, her inner connection to Lilith troubled him.

'What's up?' she asked him with a creased brow.

'I want Henderson to suffer, but Caster is aware of me. He's far more than a psychic, and I don't know what to do with him yet.'

'He found our hideout, and they got the Henderson girl back.' Brian sat back in his armchair, puffing on his cigarette. 'Even shot Thomas.'

'He must have had help.'

'Where does this leave us? We can't get the money from Henderson, just revenge.' Brian shrugged.

Mark nodded with a smile and drank his tea. 'I've got Jonas checking out his place to make the hits, and then I'll decide what to do.' He looked at Bradley sitting next to Brian. 'What of Thomas?'

'He is still in hospital, and it will take him months to recover.'

'Now we have Jonas. We don't need him.' Mark made a dismissive wave of his hand.

'Maggie and the boys have restraining orders until what happened at the site is resolved. Since they were the victims, found tied and gagged, their lawyers will manage to get them out on bail until the hearing.' He shrugged with a frown. 'Maggie wants to leave the UK before the hearing. You know she has a retreat in Barbados.'

'Can you arrange that?' Mark asked.

'It would mean using a false passport and visa. I know someone who can sort that.'

'Also, have Karl and Mike return to the States. They can start working on the Washington project. Brian has the details of the operation.'

The doorbell rang, and Pirtsha got up to check the door cam. 'It's Jonas,' she told Mark.

'Let him in. I want to know the situation at Henderson's place.' He turned to Brian. 'And I want my witches and Luther here.'

***

Pirtsha had a long shower in the morning, enjoying the hot water running over her pale flesh. The pleasant sensation thrilled her nervous system with joy. Drying her thin body, she looked in the full-length mirror and shuddered. Having a human form still felt strange, but she liked the experience and was fascinated by living in this physical world. After dressing in a blue smock that hung loosely on her, she brushed her auburn hair back into a ponytail.

'Pirtsha,' Brian called her from the lounge.

She went in to find him stubbing out a cigarette. He puffed out smoke, and she sensed his concern.

'Teresa, Penelope and Luther will be here tomorrow,' he told her. 'But Lesley has been in hospital and is not well. Can you let Mark know?'

'I will.' She glanced at him, and he smiled at her with a glint in his eye.

Mark was at his desk in the study, reading some old manuscripts.

'Two witches and Luther will be here tomorrow, but Lesley is ill.'

He looked at her with a frown. 'What's the matter with her?'

'I don't know. Brian said she's recovering after being in hospital.'

'Well, I need her and the group to do a power rite. Take a cab and see if you can persuade her to come. Use your magic and give her a boost.'

'Yes, I will leave now.' She took out her phone and called a taxi. She liked going out alone, seeing people and enjoying this fascinating physical world.

***

Pirtsha pressed the doorbell and heard it sounding inside the apartment.

Lesley opened the door and frowned at her. 'Hi, darling. Did Mark send you?'

Pirtsha nodded with a smile. Lesley wore a nightie and looked like she had just gotten out of bed. Her greying brown hair was uncombed, and she had bags under her watery blue eyes.

'Mark wants you and the group to form a power circle.'

'A power rite! Why?'

'I don't know.'

'I heard about the botched kidnapping. What a mess. That's never happened before. Anyway, come in, darling. I'll make us some tea, and you can tell me what happened.'

'Of course.' She entered and looked around. The apartment felt lived-in and was untidy. 'It's a nice place.'

'It's my home while I'm in the UK. I like it here. Don't mind the mess, dear. I've been ill recently.'

'I only found out today.' She smiled, tilting her head. 'Mark thought you might need a healing?'

'That would be lovely. You have that magic touch being Lilith's child.'

'I enjoy being me and living in this fascinating world.'

'Lilith and Mark created you. And he conditioned you to be his slave, unlike your mother, who even spurned Adam's authority.'

'Mark is my lord, but I have free will.'

'I've sensed that independence is growing in you. Have you serviced Mark or anyone sexually?'

Pirtsha blushed. 'I'm still a virgin. I feel Mark and the other men are afraid to have sex with me.'

Lesley chuckled. 'They sense the Otherness between your legs. Your alien spirit is believed to consume their lovers. That's why they're afraid of you. But they also lust after you because your fanny acts like a Venus Flytrap. Enticing them in to be consumed.'

'You tease.' She giggled. 'Mother created me this way, which links her to me in this world. I do feel that sexual ache, but I have control of myself, and I don't want to hurt anyone.'

'You are one strange creature, Pirtsha, one of a kind. Like a Succubus, your mother can feed on their souls during sex. Anyway, darling, I'll return with you if you give me that healing boost. I owe Mark for helping me out financially.'

'Of course. Sit in the chair. You will be unconscious for a while.'

Pirtsha placed her hands on either side of Lesley's head and released a stream of conditioned etheric energy. Lesley sagged into a deep, healing sleep. During the session, Pirtsha experienced Lesley's fierce sense of independence and freedom, even from Mark. She liked the feeling of being free. It reminded her of Lilith, who was free and independent from everyone. After ten minutes, Pirtsha removed her hands and waited for Lesley to recover. Of all Mark's occult group, she liked Lesley the best.

Chapter Eight

E dward shuddered and opened his eyes when Lucy called him. He had been dozing in an armchair in the study and woke with a start. 'Yeah?' He sat up.

'We're ready in the lounge,' she said. 'But Martin wants to see you first. Oh, here he is.'

'Got some feedback from Harry,' Martin said and sat opposite. 'The apartment is not that secure. There have been some people coming and going. I got a few pics. One is Brian Kempt, and another is that policeman, Bradley. One guy.' He showed him the tablet. 'Looks like the guy we got on CCTV snooping around here. Harry did a check on him. His name's Roger Saliman from Israel. Unfortunately, he's an assassin. Calls himself Jonas.'

'Better warn the others.' He flicked through the pictures. There were several images of a skinny woman who looked familiar. 'Who's this?'

'Got nothing on her or the other woman she returned with.' He frowned. 'The little woman looks ill, sort of anorexic even.'

Edward handed the tablet back. 'It's Jonas who bothers me. He could be out there waiting.' He glanced at Lucy and remembered the car bomb that had killed his wife. 'We must take precautions.'

Edward found them sitting in a circle in the lounge, waiting for him. As he entered the circle, they started chanting the Omm.

'You've got the hang of this,' he said with approval. 'I'm going to do another projection.' He sat cross-legged and closed his eyes.

It took a while to align the chakras, prepare his intent, and bond the group. Then, he focused on the crown centre above the top of his head and rose out of his body. A sense of exhilaration flushed his astral form, and he enjoyed the intense livingness of everything in the astral world. Thinking of the penthouse, he suddenly found himself on the roof garden. A group of people were sitting outside, drinking and smoking. He hovered near enough to hear them talking and recognised Inspector Bradley.

'I thought you were going to wait,' Bradley said.

'Mark wants the hits done before we return to the States next week,' a woman said. 'He's going to use a ritual to distract the men while making the mother and daughter either leave the house or enter the garden together.'

'Are you okay with that, Jonas?' Bradley asked.

'Sure, I'll be staked out monitoring the place. And I can be ready for them out the front or in the garden. I just need to get them together.'

'The others will be here tomorrow,' a man said.

'I hear Luther will be coming,' the woman muttered. 'He gives me the creeps.'

Edward froze as the strange woman came outside and stared directly at him. There was an energy exchange with a sense of familiarity for a long, intense moment. While lingering in her alien presence, Mark came outside, and she abruptly spiked Edward. Suddenly, he was back in the circle, covered in sweat with his heart pounding. She had repulsed him, and the impact had broken his projection.

'Wow!' He started to get up, then slumped on the carpet, physically drained with only a vague recall of what happened.

'That is one powerful female,' he thought as Lucy and Martin helped him to stand.

'Well?' Lucy asked.

He rubbed his forehead and eyes. 'I heard some of them talking of using a ritual and sending Jonas here, but I got repulsed, and it distorted the details. We're dealing with a group of occultists working with Skully, which means they're very dangerous.' He cringed, thinking, *'What the fuck have I got Lucy and myself into?'*

***

In her bedroom, Sophia shivered, feeling vulnerable, and turned to Alex. 'I feel afraid knowing that assassin is out there.'

'Yeah, but fear comes with a buzz, right?'

'A bittersweet buzz. I wish this were over, but I like the group sessions with Edward.'

'I've never experienced anything like that.' Alex made a little smile, then shrugged. 'It's changed me, and I think the others, especially Vincent. There's something very strange about Edward.'

'I think he's like a Jedi knight!' She chuckled, 'And I'm so glad you're here, Alex.' She bit her lip. Should she make the first move to test the waters? Caution to the wind, she hugged Alex, enjoying the contact with her strong, muscular body.

Alex brushed the hair from Sophia's face, and their eyes met. Sophia melted, feeling her heart flutter while trembling.

'You are a warrior, Alex, and...and I'm attracted to you. I hope you don't mind?' She held her breath, hoping she wouldn't be rejected.

'I've noticed, and I do like you.' She smiled nervously, making a little sigh. 'But your dad employs me, and I can't get involved. You understand?'

'Do you like girls?'

'Hey, I've trained and worked with men since leaving school, and they treat me as one of the guys. I did have a girlfriend in the force, but—' She looked away for a moment. 'Her name was Chloe. We were ambushed on manoeuvres, and she didn't survive. I tried to save her, but she died in my arms.'

'Oh, God. I am so sorry. That's terrible.' Sophia sagged and put her hand on her heart.

'Life goes on.' She shrugged, making a sad face, then smiled. 'You're a beautiful princess, but I'm just a grunt soldier, well below your league.'

'You are lovely, Alex. And I would like to get to know you in that way.' She took a deep breath. 'I had a girlfriend at school who reminds me of you. She was an excellent gymnast. We had a great time for a while, then her parents moved back to South America, and I never saw her again.' She made a little moan recalling their short love affair, then chuckled, remembering when they were caught frolicking in the showers. Looking at Alex, she felt a warm glow, then gave her a saucy smile and a wink.

'This could get me fired, but who knows?' Alex raised her eyebrows, and her eyes sparkled. Then, glancing out the window, she suddenly pulled Sophia away and used her communicator. 'Vincent, I gotta suspicious movement, middle attic window adjoining house. Looked like someone was using a spotter-scope.'

'I've got one of our cam-eyes on those attic windows,' Vincent's voice sounded from her communicator. 'I'll check the recordings. Over and out.'

'Let's join the others,' Alex said.

Sophia took Alex's arm, sensing her concern. 'I feel afraid.'

'Hey, I'm here to look after my Jedi princess.' She smiled and blew her a kiss.

***

Edward entered the study, and Vincent showed him the image of someone using a scope in one of the attic windows.

'We think it could be Jonas. That window overlooks the back and side of the property and most of the garden. It's a good vantage point.'

Edward went over to see the attic windows. They were all shut and dark. Closing his eyes, he focused his remote viewing and scanned the attics. An image briefly appeared of a man sitting on a camp bed, talking on a phone.

'I sense someone is there. He's alone, and the property feels empty.'

'That's Ronald Meakin's place,' Sir John said. 'It's up for sale. Well overpriced, and it's been on the market for over seven months.'

'I'd better check it out,' Martin said.

'I'll come with you and watch your back.' Craig stood and handed his military tablet to Alex.

'Can you use body cams so we can watch?' Lucy asked.

'Sure, Alex will be monitoring us.'

'You can access the house from my garden,' Sir John told Martin. 'There's a low garden wall behind the garage.'

'Better get geared up,' Martin said and left with Craig.

Again, Edward scanned the attic with remote viewing and got a brief impression that the man was eating a sandwich and waiting.

Vincent and Alex sat at the antique desk, using military tablets to monitor Martin and Craig's body cams. Sophia and Lucy joined them to watch the live feeds.

'They're almost there,' Sophia said. 'But not using the back door.'

'The doors could be rigged to alert Jonas,' Alex said.

'Silent mode, guys,' Martin's voice sounded from the tablet.

'They're going through a window in the back,' Lucy said.

'Heading upstairs,' Sophia added.

'Martin has reached the stairs to the attic, and the door is open. He's waiting for Craig.' Lucy looked at Edward. 'They're almost there.'

Edward closed his eyes. As he focused his remote viewing, he got an impression of a man behind some crates with a machine pistol in his hand.

'I think he's waiting for them,' Edward said urgently.

'Martin, Jonas knows you're there,' Alex whispered into his cam feed.

'Fuck,' Martin hissed.

Edward viewed the open loft door on Martin's video feed and saw a projectile fired inside. A moment later, it exploded, filling the loft with suffocating smoke. Suddenly, a man dived out of the room with his hand over his mouth and fired a machine pistol at Craig, rolled on the floor and fired at Martin. The video blurred, followed by the sound of muffled gunfire.

'Lost Craig's video!' Lucy shouted.

'And Martin's,' Edward said. 'We'd better get over there.' As he was about to leave, Martin's video came on with the image of Jonas on the floor. He had been shot in the head. Then, Craig appeared on the tablet. He was on the floor, doubled up and groaning.

'We smoked him out, and he attacked us,' Martin told them. 'Craig's been shot up, but I got the guy. Need a hand to get them out of here.'

'We're on our way,' Vincent said, motioning to Alex.

***

Martin returned in the early evening and updated Edward and the others in the study.

'Craig's in a private hospital being treated for two bullet wounds. His ballistic vest saved him, and he will recover. I had the body of Jonas discreetly disposed of by some people I know in the East End. His weapons and personal things I had dumped.'

'You did well,' Edward said, relieved that Jonas was no longer a threat. 'And you have some interesting contacts.'

'You missed dinner,' Audrey said. 'Would you like Susan to make you something?'

'I picked up a McDonald's on the way back, but a cup of tea would be great.'

'I'm curious about these people in the East End,' Sir John said with a frown.

'They run a small bakery with an oven that can reduce a body to ash in ninety minutes. I waited till it was done. It cost seventeen grand.'

'My butler will reimburse you,' Sir John said.

'I feel much better knowing Jonas is no longer a threat.' Sophia breathed a sigh of relief.

'He was here to kill some of us, and he shot Craig.' Edward exhaled thoughtfully. Skully had lost his hitman, but he was still a serious threat.

'You look worried, Dad,' Lucy said.

'Yeah, something doesn't feel right.'

***

'Thank you for coming, my old friend.' Mark stood and welcomed Luther as he entered the lounge. Luther was a short, stocky man with a shaved head and dangling pentagon earrings that he frequently twiddled. He wore grey corduroy trousers and a worn leather jacket.

'I thought our group meeting would be in the States next week. Anyway, you look good, and you're staying young. I see your moonchild has matured into a formidable woman. I remember her in an incubator. Her physical development was phenomenal. Is she still a virgin?'

'Yes. Would you like the honour of being the first?'

Luther chuckled with a glint in his eye. 'I am no fool. She has inherited her mother's nature and could suck the life out of any man, even you. Tell me again, what was it like merging with Lilith?'

He made a face and shuddered at the memory. 'She ripped me apart to extract the seed from my life force. It was a painful experience that I never want to repeat.'

'Yes, but it enhanced your being. And it keeps you young.'

'I still age, but more slowly.'

'So, why have you called this group meeting?'

'I want to use a power rite to deal with some loose ends.'

'Is Henderson one of those loose ends?'

'Of course! He got my brother killed, and I've waited years to exact my revenge. But Caster got involved and screwed up the operation.'

'Edward Caster is just a has-been psychic. What's the problem?' He shrugged, and his eyes narrowed.

'He is far more than a psychic, and he's repelled me twice, once while using a stealth Djinn.'

'Hmm, then it should be an interesting power ritual.'

Mark's phone buzzed. It was Bradley.

'The boys and Maggie are back at their hotel waiting for the travel docs. But I can't get through to Jonas. I've tried both his phones and called his hotel.'

'He's probably having a nap before the ritual. Try again later and let me know.'

'Will do.' He disconnected.

Mark put his phone down and sighed, annoyed that Jonas wasn't ready.

Pirtsha entered, nodded at Luther and faced Mark. 'Penelope has arrived, and she wants to see you privately.'

'Okay, I'll see her in the study.' He smiled at Luther and said, 'I'll leave you in Pirtsha's capable hands.'

Luther raised an eyebrow and shook his head.

***

Mark kissed Penelope when she entered the study. 'Thanks for coming. You look great.' He smiled and winked at her.

'I intuited you needed me and was coming here when Brian called.'

'You're my love, and we go back a long way.' He enjoyed her physical presence and the memories of their young love affair. Though in her fifties, she was still attractive and had recovered from having cosmetic surgery in Belgium. Her hair was now blonde, and she wore a purple, low-cut outfit that enhanced her bust and cleavage.

Frowning, she narrowed her eyes. 'But I grew old, and you've remained in your prime.'

'You could have joined me.'

Pulling away, she shook her head. 'No. The sacrifice was too great.'

'I believe you're still a Christian deep down.'

'Maybe, yes, I was brought up in a convent. And though I have done questionable things using the dark art, I still value my soul.' She made a sad face at him.

'Ha! I knew it. And I still love you.'

'Mark, you're incapable of love. Except love for yourself.'

'Love is transitory, Penelope, as is the human soul.' He felt a pang of regret and turned away.

She put her arm around him. 'Nothing can be done about the past. So, what are we here for?'

'I have an old and a new score to settle.'

'And you need to use a power rite? Is that really necessary?'

He nodded with a grin. 'Empowering the group before we leave for the States will prepare us for the Washington project.'

***

Mark and his group were finishing their meal in the lounge when his phone buzzed. It was Bradley.

'Hi, Mark. Nothing on Jonas.'

'Damn it! Never mind, I'm about to summon a Djinn, and I'll find out what's going on.' He disconnected and switched off his phone. He tried to connect with Jonas using remote viewing but failed. Puzzled by the lack of contact, a nagging sensation bothered him.

'Gather around and create a circle,' he told his group.

Once settled, Mark connected psychically with each of them. Then, he intoned an invocation to summon a Djinn entity. The sound of wind rushing in trees swirled around the room, and the atmosphere became cold and electrically charged. The dark, shimmering form of a humanoid Djinn gradually materialised between Mark and the others. Its black eyes glared intensely at each of them. Then it faced Mark and breathed foul odour at him.

Gripping the Djinn, Mark commanded it to enter and scan Henderson's home. There, he found most of the people in the lounge. Looking around, he saw Edward tense and glance in his direction. Swiftly, he pulled away from them to stay concealed in the shadows. Thinking of Jonas, he called him several times, but there was no response.

'Where is Jonas?' he asked.

The Djinn scanned for several minutes, then replied, 'He is not in this world.'

'No! How?'

'Unknown, see fire, and his spirit entangled in netherworld.'

Shocked by the revelation, Mark returned to his group and dismissed the Djinn.

'Jonas is dead!' he snapped with a shake of his head, then took a long, deep breath. 'Now I'm fucking, fucking mad. Pirtsha, empower the group and open a portal into Otherness.'

Pirtsha stood behind him, placed her hands on either side of his head, and released a surge of conditioned etheric energy to connect with the Dark Current.

Mark felt his body shudder as his nervous system and mind became enflamed with dark energy. He paused to stabilise the intensity of this altered state, then focused his thoughts and summoned one of the dragon Djinn entities from this alien realm. These powerful, dangerous beings like to experience the warmth of the physical world, but they need a willing human conduit to come through.

'Link with me and witness,' Mark told his group.

They gasped when the alien manifested through Mark and filled the room with its disturbing presence. He chuckled, gripping the powerful Djinn, and used the command for it to enter Henderson's house.

***

Lucy handed Edward a cup of tea and sat beside him in the lounge.

'I feel a bit on edge,' she told him.

Sensing her concern, he abruptly stood as a grotesque entity began manifesting in the room. Its humming, silvery form shimmered, and its black eyes scanned each of them. An icy breeze washed over Edward. He focused and thrust a power spike at it, but the entity absorbed the energy and smothered Lucy. She screamed and fell unconscious. Then, Audrey staggered and fell as it smothered her. Abruptly, the entity was gone, and the room became cold and silent with the fading energy of Otherness.

Holding Lucy, he placed his fingers on her neck and felt a weak pulse. He shook her limp body and called her, but she didn't wake up.

'What the fuck just happened?' Martin asked, helping Audrey into an armchair. She was unconscious, and Alex tended to her.

'We were attacked, and I couldn't stop it,' Edward snapped. Again, he tried to wake Lucy, but she was unresponsive. Numb and shocked, he picked her up and carried her to her room. With tears in his eyes, he held Lucy's hand. She was lying on the bed, her eyes closed and her mouth partly open. Her breathing was shallow, and her skin was pale.

Closing his eyes, he probed her psychically to find her spirit had departed. Her body was like an empty husk. His sense of failure at losing Lucy tore through his mind and heart. He had lost his wife to terrorists, and now Skully had taken his daughter. He should have protected her, but he underestimated Skully's occult powers. If only he hadn't got involved with this damn kidnapping, she would still be here. Focusing, he reasoned that since her body was still alive, there might be a way for her soul to return.

'What happened to her?' Sophia asked, pale-faced.

'I'm not sure. I'll need to do some work with the group.' He looked up at her with a forced smile. 'How is your mother?'

'Sleeping now. Thank God Alex was a field medic in the forces.'

'You like her, don't you?'

'Yeah, I do.' She blushed.

'When your mother wakes, can everyone assemble in the lounge? I want to see if I can help Lucy.'

She hugged him and left.

Vincent entered, looked at Lucy and let out a deep sigh. 'How is she?'

'She's in a coma, and I can't connect with her.' He pulled the sheet up to her neck and tucked her in. 'Her body is alive, but her spirit is gone.'

'Gone? Is she dead?' he asked, and his eyes welled up.

'I don't know. But I'll try to find out in the next session.' He sensed Vincent's feelings for Lucy, smiled, and gave him a pat on the back.

***

Edward viewed the sombre-looking group in the lounge and went over to Audrey.

'How are you now?'

She made a weak smile. 'Still here, thanks to Alex.'

'Good. This session will help restore you.' He moved into the centre of the circle and faced each of them. 'I want to find out what happened to Lucy, and it means using occult knowledge. So far, we have used the group as an energy battery to aid my projections. Now, I need your participation, and it will change you at a deep level. You will never be the same again.'

'Change us in what way?' Martin asked.

'You will see and awaken to a greater view, which will alter your understanding of life.' Looking around at them, he said, 'If any of you do not want to participate, then wait in the study until it is over. Think about this now because there is no turning back.'

He left them to check on Lucy and use the bathroom. The loss of his beloved daughter and the guilt of not protecting her weighed heavily on his mind. He had to get her back. There must be a way.

When he returned, they were waiting for him, except for Michael and Susan, who stood by the door to the study.

'We would rather not be involved, sir,' he said. 'However, we will always be here to serve you.'

'A wise decision, Michael,' Edward said, smiled at Susan, and entered the circle.

Edward sat cross-legged on the floor and started the Omm chant. As the humming filled the room, he intoned an invocation to power the group and opened his mind to the memories of his childhood when he encountered the realm of Otherness.

As the energy washed through them, the group gasped, stopped chanting, and remained in a state of intense awareness.

'Do not be afraid,' Edward said. 'You are on the Edge of Otherness. A cosmic realm so vast it is infinite. Do not let your mind wander because you can get lost in that vastness. Always remain as a group with me as your guide. Hold fast now, my friends.' Using a facet of the knowledge to empower his projection, he focused on Skully's penthouse and was suddenly standing on the roof garden in his enhanced astral form.

He could sense Skully with some people inside and was about to enter when the woman came out and sat on one of the chairs under the pergola. Intrigued, he hovered over to get a better impression of her. She was a small, thin woman, probably in her late twenties or early thirties.

'I see you,' she said, looking up at him.

'Can you hear me?'

'Of course. Why are you here?'

'Your master, Skully, has taken my daughter's soul.'

'Not Mark. It was the dragon entity that took her beyond the Abyss. I broke the rite to stop it taking the other woman.'

'How can I get her back?'

'You can't. She is lost forever.'

'No! There must be a way—'

'Pirtsha,' a man called from the open patio doors. 'Mark wants you, now!'

She got up, shook her head at Edward, and went inside.

Edward felt his astral form shudder, and he was abruptly back in the circle, covered in sweat.

He let out a heavy sigh, his heart aching. Would he ever see Lucy again? Looking around at the astonished people, he forced a smile. They had bonded during the session, and he was pleased. From the knowledge he had suppressed since childhood, he drew into his being the energy of Otherness, then released it as a vision of that vastness to strengthen the group.

For a timeless moment, through Edward, the group mind touched the cosmic realm of Otherness, and there were gasps of awe. The silence in the room lingered for a long time before Martin spoke.

'I have seen beyond. I'm used to living on the edge, but that has opened my mind.'

'I can't believe I've just seen another world, another existence,' Vincent said, wiping the sweat from his face.

'You said it would change us,' Sir John said, holding Audrey's hand. 'And it has altered my perception of this physical world. There is so much more out there and within.'

'What of Lucy?' Sophia asked.

He sagged with a shake of his head. 'I encountered Skully's woman. She was aware of my astral body, and we communicated. She said Lucy's soul is entrapped in the realm of Otherness and cannot return.'

'What the hell is she?' Alex asked.

Edward made a little shrug and frowned. 'I'm not sure, but from the knowledge, a moonchild is a hybrid, half-human and half-Djinn.'

'Djinn?' Audrey queried.

'They are beings from Otherness. Some are nasty entities and hostile to our world and us. In ancient times, I believe there was a war between them and the guardians of this world.'

'Guardians?' Martin frowned.

'They exist, but they don't interfere.'

'Is there any way you can help Lucy?' Alex asked.

Edward sighed. Using his psychic ability had caused the death of his wife, and now Lucy was gone. His body twisted, and he groaned. He had failed the two people he loved with all his being. And now there was only deep regret and endless suffering.

'Are you okay?' Alex asked him.

He nodded and focused. 'Maybe that woman knows what to do.' He looked at the others. 'Let's have a break. Then I'll try again to connect with her.'

'I felt we're dealing with transcendental states tinged with forbidden knowledge,' Vincent said.

'You have intuited correctly.' Edward sensed that Vincent was developing psychic awareness. 'We are dealing with the Night Side of Eden. A path that utilises the wisdom of the reptilian being who guards the fire of eternal life and who influenced Lilith and Eve.'

'As a Master Mason,' Sir John said. 'I know of this ancient path, but no one can access that forbidden knowledge.'

'No one except Edward,' Sophia said. 'He is our Jedi Knight!'

'A rather dark knight,' Martin said with a hint of a smile.

Chapter Nine

PART THREE

Pirtsha refused to open the door to Otherness for Mark. When she interacted with Edward, she felt his grief at losing his daughter, whom he loved. And his unusual presence intrigued her.

'I'm your fucking lord!' Mark raged at her. 'I created you to obey me!'

Pirtsha glanced at Lesley, who smiled with a nod of approval at her defiance.

'You will do as I tell you.' He insisted, pointing at her.

'You don't need me.' She backed away from him, and her eyes flared with intensity.

'Go to your room. You will stay there until you come to your senses and do as I command.'

She entered the small bedroom, and Mark locked her in.

Sitting on the bed, she shook with annoyance at the way he treated her. She had been conditioned to obey Mark as her lord, but now she felt disturbed by his ruthlessness. He was more like Lilith than she was. In Edward, she had sensed a balance between the light and the dark forces. It was an extremely rare balance in either world, and like Mark, he was an occultist.

Lying on the bed, she closed her eyes and relaxed. After a while, she sensed Mark and the others performing a complex rite using the Djinn. Thinking of Edward, she wondered about him. The witches talked about his TV psychic shows. She puckered, recalling her feeling of seeing his dream body. Curiously, she focused her intent and called him repeatedly.

'Who are you?' Edward eventually responded.

'I saw your dream body on the roof garden,' she thought. *'My name is Pirtsha.'*

'I'm Edward. You know about my daughter. I have to get her back.'

'It's not possible. I'm so sorry. I broke the rite to stop the demon from taking any more souls, but—'

The bedroom door opened, and Mark entered.

'I want you, now!' He held out his hand. 'Come with me.'

She sensed his concern. 'What's happened?'

In the lounge, she found Lesley on the sofa, having an epileptic fit. Immediately, she went over and placed the palms of her hands on either side of Lesley's head and streamed calming energy into her nervous system. After a few minutes, Lesley's shaking stopped, and she breathed a sigh of relief before opening her eyes and being helped to sit up.

'Thank you, darling.' She touched Pirtsha's face affectionately, then frowned at Mark. 'I told you to pull back and not force the fucking Djinn. It attacked me because you lost control!'

'It won't happen again. Not now we have Pirtsha back with us.' He looked at her and smiled, but his eyes were cold.

***

'That woman, Pirtsha, briefly made contact with me,' Edward told the group. 'And I got some curious impressions from her. She feels trapped, like a slave to Skully.'

'What's she like?' Audrey asked.

'From my projections, she looked normal but seemed undernourished and skinny.' Edward closed his eyes, recalling his psychic contact with her. 'But...and this is strange. She has an alien soul in a human body with a female mind. Her name is Pirtsha.'

'Freaky,' Sophia said. 'I don't think I want to see her.'

'I would like to meet her,' Edward said. 'I feel she could help me find Lucy.'

'We know where she is.' Martin raised his brow. 'It's just a thought, but could we abduct her? I mean, they abducted Sophia.'

Edward chuckled. 'Pirtsha is not someone easy to abduct. That alien in her could be seriously dangerous. And there's Skully and his group. However, it's worth thinking of a strategy.'

'Can you reconnect with her?' Alex asked.

'I can try.' He sat in one of the armchairs and closed his eyes. It was easy now to focus on his psychic awareness. He thought of Pirtsha and called her several times, but there was no response. 'I can't connect. She seems preoccupied.'

'I still have Harry's people watching the penthouse,' Martin said. 'And we know the woman goes out. We could arrange for her abduction.'

'Interesting idea.' Vincent joined them. 'Like a black op.'

'You work on that,' Edward said. 'I'm going to check on Lucy's body.'

'Alex is looking after her,' Sophia said. 'I'll come with you.'

***

'I want to see what's happening at Henderson's place,' Mark said, motioning for his group to settle around him in the lounge. He was annoyed by Pirtsha's disobedience and would have to recondition her to break her mother's influence. He would deal with her later. 'Hopefully, they're grieving,' he said with a smile.

'Are you using a Djinn to view them?' Penelope asked.

'Yeah, it gives me more control and helps me stay in the shadows.'

Pirtsha stood near his chair, and Brian, Luther, Penelope and Lesley completed the group. Mark closed his eyes and linked them into his magnetic aura before using an invocation to summon a stealth Djinn.

For several minutes, the atmosphere in the group grew to an electrical intensity. Gradually, the Djinn manifested in a grotesque, shimmering humanoid form. Its black eyes flared, and the room filled with alien energy. Mark gripped the Djinn and commanded it to be inside Henderson's house. A sensation of being pulled followed, and they were hovering in the lounge, masked by a stealth mist.

Mark scanned the room silently, then froze, seeing that Henderson's wife was alive. Moving around the house, he found Edward's comatose daughter with two women and a man by the bed. He was about to scan the study when Edward appeared and occultly repulsed the Djinn.

'Fuck!' Mark groaned. He was back in the penthouse, the Djinn was gone, and the group energy had dissipated.

'How did Edward kick us out?' Brian asked in a weak voice.

'He used the knowledge,' Pirtsha said and puckered.

'Knowledge?' Penelope questioned.

'I felt his thrust from the Night Side. He wounded the Djinn.'

'That's impossible,' Luther said, shaking his head. 'You can't harm a Djinn.'

Mark had seen the Djinn hurt by Edward's energy spike but said nothing. Edward had grown in power, and that bothered him.

'I've had enough,' Lesley said and stood. 'I've done my part. Now I want to go home. I've been ill and need to rest.'

'Fine, Pirtsha will call a taxi for you.' Mark dismissed her with a wave, annoyed by her leaving. He felt anger burning in his stomach, but he contained the emotion.

'I think we need to chill out for the night,' Penelope said. 'I feel physically drained from that session.'

'Me too,' Brian added and lit up a cigarette.

'Well, I'm fine,' Luther said, twiddling one of his dangling earrings. 'You fancy a brandy and some online gambling?' he asked Mark, taking out his iPad.

'Why not? It'll take my mind off this bloody mess.'

***

In the morning, Edward looked up when Martin entered the lounge, smiling.

'Harry just called,' Martin said. 'The woman has left the penthouse. He's got a tail on her, and it looks like she's gone shopping.'

'Interesting. I want to meet her away from Skully.'

'Time we get there; she might be on her way back.'

'I want to be there when she returns.' He stood and buttoned his jacket. 'John, you're in charge of the group.' Then to Martin, 'Let's get going.'

'Might be best to head for the penthouse and wait there.'

'You look excited.'

Martin chuckled. 'Let's go.'

***

Edward saw the taxi pull up outside the block of flats, and he got out of Martin's vehicle. The woman paid the driver and picked up her shopping. She was about to enter the building when Edward confronted her.

'Pirtsha, I'm Edward.' He felt a moment of awe in her dark, alien presence. She was a strange-looking woman with a fleshless face and dark, intense eyes.

She glared at him, and her eyes narrowed. 'What do you want?'

'I want my daughter back from the Abyss. And you can help me.'

'No, I can't help, and she is lost forever. Go away, or Mark will kill you.'

He brushed his fingertips across her forehead and temple, releasing the energy of compliance. She gasped, mouth open, and stepped back.

'You have the knowledge.'

'Pirtsha, come with me and gain your freedom from Mark Skully. I can protect and look after you. And you will be a free spirit in this world. Do you want to be free?'

She glanced up at the penthouse and frowned. 'Free...a free spirit! He will never let me go. No, I am his child. He needs me and will come for me.'

'I know, and I will be ready. You can trust me, Pirtsha. Touch my mind and see. I am connected to the Night Side of Eden.'

Her face paled. She dropped her shopping and stepped back with her hand on her mouth. 'That's impossible,' she murmured, her eyes glazed with intensity. 'It's a forbidden realm where even angels cannot enter.'

'Pirtsha, I hide nothing from you. I must get my daughter's soul back and need your help. In return, I have the knowledge to free and protect you from Skully. Enter my mind, and you will see. Then you can decide to stay with him or come with me.'

'If you try to entrap or condition me, I will seriously hurt you.'

She reached up and held his head in the palms of her hands. He felt her penetrating energy scanning his mind and memories. When the memory of his childhood connection to Eden surfaced, she gasped, glaring at him wide-eyed.

He swooned as her otherworldly essence flooded his mind. At that moment, something primordial within her made contact with his inner self, leaving him transfixed until she withdrew her small, perspiring hands and broke the connection.

'You've entered that forbidden realm and survived!' She picked up her shopping bags. 'Because of your link to Eden, my mother wants me to join you. I don't know why because Mark is going to be furious. You don't know what he is capable of.' She paused, gazing into his eyes. 'I will go with you, but Mark will come for me and want to destroy you.'

He wanted to speak and thank her, but her energy from the mind meld lingered with an uncomfortable intensity. He frowned. She had a disturbing yet stimulating presence, unlike anyone he had ever known. She was a strange little woman with a dark alien soul.

***

Sophia checked on Lucy and found Alex setting up an intravenous drip in her arm. She leaned over, brushed the hair from Lucy's pale face, and stifled a sob.

'Will she survive?' Sophia asked, feeling a pang of despair.

'I can keep her body alive, but Edward said her soul is in that other world. Maybe if we—' Her phone buzzed. She answered it, then said, 'That was Martin. Edward has the woman. They didn't have to abduct her.'

'I wonder what she's like, a woman with an alien spirit?'

'They're on their way back, so we'll see soon enough.'

'Let's go down and tell the others.'

Sophia found her father, Audrey, and Vincent in the lounge, having tea.

'They'll soon be here with that alien woman,' Sophia told them excitedly.

'We know,' Vincent said. 'Edward just called me and said Pirtsha agreed to come with him.'

'Pirtsha is a strange name.'

'I looked it up on the Internet,' Audrey said. 'Pirtsha is another name for Lilith, Adam's first wife, who rejected him.'

'I didn't know Adam had a wife before Eve,' Alex said. 'What happened to her?'

'After refusing to obey Adam, she was punished and cast out of this world,' Audrey replied, then stood when the doorbell sounded.

After a few minutes, the butler entered with Edward, Martin, and a woman.

Sophia focused on her and held her breath. Pirtsha was a small, pale-faced woman with auburn hair pulled back. Her red dress appeared too large for her petite body, and her black leather jacket was unzipped. Sophia exhaled in relief as she realised Pirtsha was a normal adult woman. However, there was something slightly unsettling about her presence, especially when she gazed at Sophia for an intense moment.

'I would like to introduce Pirtsha,' Edward said. 'She is here to help me with Lucy.'

'Welcome to my home,' Sir John said. 'My wife, Audrey, has arranged accommodation for you.'

'Thank you.' She frowned. 'I sense you're nervous, but there is no need to fear me. I'm here because of Edward.'

'I have agreed to protect her from Mark Skully.'

'Does he know she is here?' Audrey asked.

'Not yet.' Edward hugged Pirtsha, and she looked up at him and smiled. 'These people are my bonded group. I want you to get to know each other.'

'We've never met anyone like you before,' Sophia said and greeted her.

'Are you the one Mark had kidnapped?'

'I am. Fortunately, Edward and Martin rescued me.'

'Mark intended to kill you when he got the money. Even after you got away, he hired Jonas to kill you, your mother and Edward.'

'Kill me! I knew it.' Sophia scowled. 'I never trusted those abductors.'

Audrey hugged Sophia, then faced Pirtsha. 'What did he do to Lucy and me?'

'He used a power rite to summon a dragon Djinn, who stole Lucy's soul. It tried to get your soul, but I broke the rite.' She paused with a frown. 'Mark Skully is my donor father, but he is consumed with power that has corrupted him. I want to be free of his control, and Edward can help me.'

'What are these djinns?' Alex asked.

Pirtsha frowned. 'They are supernatural creatures that were expelled from this world a long time ago. Many still haunt humanity, and some can be extremely dangerous.'

'Like the one that got Lucy.' Alex shuddered.

'There are many kinds of these entities. Some are dragons and others are shapeshifters.'

'Before Skully finds out you've gone,' Edward said. 'I want us to form a circle and perform a rite.'

***

'Are you ready?' Edward asked Pirtsha. He offered his hand, and they entered the circle. 'We will perform the rite and alter your psychic signature to prevent Skully from connecting with you.'

'Is that from the knowledge?'

'It is.'

'I can energise the group for you,' she offered.

'Be my guest.'

She knelt on the carpet, facing away from him.

He placed his hands on her bony shoulders, then said, 'Do it.'

She lowered her head, and he felt her connect to the Dark Current. He stiffened as the energy flowed through him, energising the group into a powerful unity.

From the Serpent's knowledge, he used a spell to create the sheath of the snake and cast it over Pirtsha to mask her personal signature.

Drawing again from the knowledge, he used a command and opened a vista to the vastness beyond the solar system. The group gasped in awe as they experienced the shocking reality of cosmic space.

'It is done,' Edward said, breaking the circle.

'I could barely comprehend galactic space,' Martin said, rubbing his head. 'It numbed my mind, and I felt I'd touched something...something divine.'

'We were on the edge of the solar system, gazing into outer space,' Vincent said. 'I will never forget that. Wow!' He lay on the carpet and placed his hands over his eyes.

Pirtsha stood, stretched her back and smiled at everyone. 'You have the nucleus of a powerful group. And I will help you to become formidable.'

***

'Where's Pirtsha?' Mark asked Brian in the lounge.

'She went shopping this morning and should have returned by now.'

Mark closed his eyes and called her psychically. There was no response. He tried several times, then looked at Brian. 'She isn't here. Where the hell is she?'

'I don't know.' He took out his phone and called her. 'Her phone is switched off.'

'Fuck! I don't like this.'

'Could she have gone to visit Lesley? I know she was concerned about her.'

'I doubt it, but call her anyway.'

Penelope entered. 'What's the commotion?'

'Pirtsha has gone missing.'

'Are you sure? I thought she'd gone shopping.'

'So did we.'

'Has this happened before?'

Mark shook his head with a grunt. 'Never. She's always been connected to me, but now I can't even sense her.' He closed his eyes, relaxed the tension in his body, and focused his inner eye on remote viewing Pirtsha. Gradually, an image appeared of a becalmed ocean. He tried several times and got the same image. 'I don't understand. All I see is water.'

'Just a thought,' Penelope said, touching his arm. 'Could she have been drugged and abducted?'

'Who would be stupid enough to abduct her?' He dismissed the idea with a wave of his hand.

Luther entered, smoking a cigar. He puffed out a stream of smoke, then looked at Mark with a creased brow. 'Problems?'

'Pirtsha's missing. I'll need to use a Djinn to scan for her.'

'Missing? Are you serious?' He started to chuckle, then frowned and stubbed out the cigar. 'I thought she was permanently connected to you.'

'So did I.' Mark stood, gutted by her absence. He had used her for his power rituals and should have reconditioned her when she refused to obey him. He sighed and shook his head. Had she deliberately left him, or did someone abduct her?

Mark sat in his chair with Luther, Brian and Penelope in front of him.

Taking a few deep breaths, he connected psychically with them and used an invocation to empower the group. Focusing, he summoned a stealth Djinn, which manifested its disturbing alien form between them. Gripping the Djinn, he commanded it to find Pirtsha.

For ten minutes, the Djinn scanned silently.

'I cannot find Pirtsha, maybe in a mist or not in this world.'

Shocked, Mark dismissed the Djinn and closed the group.

'How can the Djinn not find her?' Penelope asked wide-eyed. 'Is Pirtsha dead?'

'No, I don't think so, but I'm not sure where she is or what's happened.'

Luther shook his head. 'Pirtsha can't just disappear. Someone else must be involved. But who?'

Mark stiffened as Edward came to mind. It didn't make sense. He shrugged, dismissing the thought, then got his phone out to call Bradley.

'I can contact the Taxi Company that Pirtsha used,' Brian said. 'Do some detective work.'

'Do it, Brian. Someone must have seen what happened to her. And keep checking her phone.'

***

Edward took Pirtsha to see Lucy's comatose body. She placed the palms of her hands on Lucy's head and closed her eyes. After a few minutes, she removed her hands and turned to Edward.

'Her cord is still alive, but she is lost. Finding the dragon Djinn who took her will be difficult. And it would mean entering Otherness beyond the Abyss.'

'Have you been in that realm?'

'Several times, like when Lilith gave me life. Then, I was incubated in the physical world and grew this human body. My growth has stabilised.'

'What happens when your body dies?'

'Mother will reabsorb my life force, and I will cease to exist.'

Edward felt a pang of sadness for her. 'Is she living through you?'

'No. I am detached from her like a satellite. Mother can't enter physical space. She had to pull Mark into her realm to create me.'

Looking at Lucy's body, he felt a pang of grief. 'Can I enter the Abyss?'

'Maybe.' She touched his arm. 'But you need to prepare first, and that's dangerous. Also, it can be difficult to return.'

'Can I find Lucy's soul?'

'It might be possible, but Edward, you could get lost in there forever!'

'I will need to access the knowledge. There is so much, and I've only scratched the surface.'

'Mark will be looking for me and will never give up. He needs me to open the Abyss safely.'

He gazed into her pale, drawn face and asked, 'How can I enter the Abyss?'

'You will have to merge with me and may not survive!' She touched his left temple with her fingertips.

He experienced an intelligent stream of knowledge from her and understood the danger of being consumed by merging with her demon nature.

'Is that the only way?' he asked with a tremor of fear.

'It is the only way I know of.' She gave him a saucy smile. 'If it works, you will become an Avatar, and we can search for Lucy's soul beyond the abyss.'

'And if it doesn't, your mother will consume my soul, and I will cease to exist.'

She hugged him, resting her head on his chest. 'That is the danger. And I have no control over that part of my demon nature.'

***

'Well?' Mark asked Brian, who had entered the roof garden carrying an iPad.

'The taxi driver said he dropped her off outside here with her shopping.' He sat and lit a cigarette. 'However, I got the janitor to let me see the CCTV recording of the front entrance.' He handed Mark the iPad with a clip from the recording. 'A man spoke to her, and she held his head for several minutes, then went with him.'

Viewing the video, Mark froze the clip on the man's face. 'Who is this guy?'

'I don't know. I've not seen him around here.'

He showed the image to Penelope, and she frowned, scrutinising the face. 'I'm not sure, but that could be Edward Caster.' She handed the iPad to Luther.

'That fucking psychic!' Mark snapped. 'Why would he want Pirtsha?'

'And why did she go with him?' Luther asked, viewing the video. 'He didn't force or abduct her. She even took her shopping.'

Mark closed his eyes and focused his psychic awareness on Pirtsha, but only a becalmed ocean appeared. He then focused on Edward and held his breath as a tumultuous waterfall flushed his awareness and drained his attention.

'Fuck! He's shielded. Where did he learn to use this advanced magic?'

'From Pirtsha, maybe?' Penelope said.

'No, she doesn't have that kind of knowledge. And I think he could be shielding her from me.'

'That would make him a practising occultist.' Luther made a face, then smiled. 'I wonder if he knows she is also like a Succubus, the consumer of souls.'

Mark chuckled at the thought. 'Let's hope he fancies her sexually.' His phone buzzed, and he took it out.

'Hi, Mark.' It was Bradley.

'Where have you been? I've called and left messages.'

'I've been fucking suspended. They're on to me over those false passports that Maggie and the boys use to break their bail. And they know I accessed some restricted files. It means there will be an inquiry.'

'I wonder if Henderson is behind this? You said he has Masonic connections.'

'Could be. I've been cold-shouldered since John got his daughter back.'

'Yeah, and now Pirtsha's gone AWOL. We think she might be with that psychic.'

'Did he abduct her?'

'We don't know. Look, I need another hitman and a private dick to stake out Henderson's place.'

'The detective is not a problem, but after Jonas disappeared, the word on the street is not good.'

'See what you can do, and let me know. And I'll double your fee for helping us.'

'Okay, thanks, Mark.' Bradley disconnected.

Mark stood. 'I want to scan Henderson's place. We'll use the Farsight ritual.'

***

'What do you think of Pirtsha?' Sophia asked the group, who were having tea in the lounge while Edward and Pirtsha were with Lucy.

'She is one strange female,' Vincent said. 'When I'm near her, I get a hard-on.'

They laughed.

'I think she's a nice person, but she needs to put on some weight,' Alex said.

'I feel uneasy with her.' Audrey scowled. 'There is something alien in her.'

Martin finished his cup of tea and raised his eyebrows. 'When I met her, I felt she was a normal woman until she gazed into my eyes, and I almost wet myself.'

'I don't know if anyone has noticed,' Sir John said, leaning back in his chair. 'But we have changed. I feel that everyone here is linked to each other. And we're all linked to Edward.'

'We are bonded and form Edward's group,' Sophia said. 'He is like our Jedi master.'

'He certainly has unique abilities,' Vincent said, smiling at Sophia. 'I guess you like the Star Wars movies.'

'Yeah, I love watching them. And I've got all the DVDS if you're interested.'

***

'Edward, the knowledge will eventually destroy your human soul,' Pirtsha said, touching his arm. He looked at her and felt deep affection. She had bonded with him during the group session, and he knew he could trust her.

'I know the sacrifice, and our path leads into the unknown.'

'Our path, Edward?'

He chuckled. 'You have joined us, Pirtsha. Unless you want to return to Mark Skully?'

'Never! His lust for power has corrupted him. He only used me to make the connection through the Abyss to Otherness.' She touched his face. 'You have helped to break his hold on me. I like being free. And I like being here with you and your group. When I saw your connection to Eden, I knew I was meant to be with you.'

'I think we should merge. It's the only way I can enter the Abyss and find Lucy.'

She lowered her head. 'Edward, my demon nature is that of a Succubus, and I have no control over it draining your life force. If we have sex, you may not survive, yet you need to merge sexually with my demon nature to be transformed. If you survive, it will bond us in spirit.' She sagged in his arms and looked up at him with tears in her eyes. 'I'm afraid of what my mother could do to you.'

'You know I'm linked to the Night Side of Eden, and we will do it in the protection of the group.' He brushed the tears from her face. 'For Lucy, I will walk on fire and sacrifice my being.' He held her head, kissed her forehead, and her body trembled in his embrace.

***

Mark simmered with anger and hatred towards Edward for abducting Pirtsha. He was determined to make them pay for what they had done. Luther, Brian, and Penelope were ready and waiting in the lounge to begin their scans to find out if Pirtsha was there. Mark psychically linked the group of four and invoked several etheric entities to energise their collective force. These beings were non-aggressive and had better stealth capabilities than the Djinn. They focused on a large crystal sphere set in a block of slate on the carpet, and Mark commanded the elementals to anchor and enhance their powered remote viewing with an Ordonic power mantra.

Mark's seeing-eye entered Henderson's house and moved through the rooms, receiving impressions. In the lounge, he paused and noticed several people sitting and talking. However, the viewing soon moved to the study, where two men were playing chess. One of them was John Henderson, who glanced around as if sensing a presence in the room.

Thinking of Pirtsha, he was drawn upstairs to a bedroom where Edward's daughter lay motionless. Suddenly, he felt a chill and turned to find Edward, who barked a command, and Mark was thrust out of the house and back to the penthouse.

He sat up and looked around. The others had also been repelled.

'What happened?' Penelope asked, sagging in her chair and nursing her head.

'Edward just kicked us out. He used a Druid power shout. Where the hell did he learn that?' He looked at the dark crystal on the floor and grunted with his fist balled.

'I sensed Pirtsha in the house but couldn't locate her,' Luther said.

'I felt the people there were occultly aware,' Brian added. 'They're not ordinary people.'

'They reminded me of a coven.' Penelope raised her brow. 'I sensed they're linked psychically and have the shining.'

Mark reluctantly agreed. 'I think we need to know more about them. And bring out the big guns.' Looking at Brian, he said, 'Also, I want Lesley and Teresa back here.'

Chapter Ten

E dward entered the lounge to find the group had arranged the circle of chairs.
'We are going to perform a power rite,' he said.

'What is a power rite?' Vincent asked. 'And what is it for?'

'Power rites involve using planetary and cosmic energies and are usually per-
formed by a group for protection. You will see the difference, and it will enhance
your view of life. While Pirtsha and I prepare, I want you to use a mantra to energise
the group.' He took in a deep breath and chanted.

'Omm mani pad mi omm, Omm mani pad mi omm...'

The group took up the chanting, and Edward left with Pirtsha.

In his room, while Pirtsha was preparing for the rite, he felt a mixture of excitement and nostalgia. He had not had sex since his wife died. Now, he was about to
have ritual sex that would involve using his chakras to stimulate kundalini energy.

He practised Kundalini meditation when he was a young man in India. He smiled
as the memory surfaced of staying in the ashram with the female sex guru, Shakti Ma.
He was there for a month and became her favourite pupil. She taught him how to
activate and use the Kundalini energy through the chakras and helped him develop
his psychic awareness. But when she discovered his connection to the Night Side of
Eden, she called him a devil and cast him out. Returning to the UK, he began his
psychic career.

'Are you sure you want to go through with this?' Pirtsha asked. She was dressed
in one of Sophia's pink bathrobes, with her hair tied back.

'Yes. I know, and I do understand the danger involved.' He pulled on a bathrobe
over his naked body. 'You are connected to Lilith, and our joining will open the door
to her influence.'

'I think you're right, Edward. Mother made me a Succubus, but I don't know
what will happen. I'm still a virgin.'

'I think our group is ready.' He took her arm, and they returned to the lounge, then entered the circle.

'You have charged the circle well,' Edward told them. 'I'm going to conjoin with Pirtsha, and you will be the witnesses of this Tantra sex ritual. Now, please continue the chanting and allow yourselves to merge with the group energy.'

Edward sat in the lotus posture on the carpet with his back straight. Pirtsha knelt before him, opened his robe, and rubbed his penis into a hard erection. Standing, she opened her robe and leaned forward to kiss his forehead and mouth. He reached between her legs and stimulated her. She trembled, placed her hands on his shoulders, and lowered herself onto his penis, making a little cry. Moving up and down, she moaned lasciviously and hugged him.

'I like this,' she whispered in his ear.

He chuckled. 'The best is yet to come. Just relax and go with the flow.'

After a few minutes, he engaged his chakras, and the kundalini energy rose up his spine and flowed into her body, stimulating her chakras. She swooned and started shaking as their internal energies merged. With the kundalini fire circulating between them, they conjoined as one energetic being. Then Edward entered her mind psychically, and their consciousness merged.

'I can't stop her consuming you, Edward!' she thought urgently, and her body started shaking violently. *'She is taking control and sucking on your life force!'*

'Let it happen,' he thought back and focused on containing Pirtsha's Succubus nature with the Serpent's knowledge. He felt rushes of stimulating energy throughout his body as they held each other. At that moment, he saw the complexity of her inner being. She was like a free spirit trapped by the influence of Mark and her mother's conditioning. He realised that Pirtsha needed balance to stabilise her independence, and he knew how to help her achieve a sense of freedom even from Lilith. As the insight faded, he enhanced her with his sense of independence.

Suddenly, a shock wave of heavy energy hit him, and they were alone on a narrow, wind-swept plateau. He looked into the infinity of dark matter surrounding them and was mentally stunned by its vastness.

'This is the Abyss,' she said, clinging to him. 'It's a neutral place where two realms meet. Be careful. If the wind takes you, there is no return.'

'I sense the Otherness out there. It's a cosmic reality.'

'While our bodies are sexually entwined, we are conjoined in spirit. Do not be afraid. Wait! Oh no, she's coming through me!'

He felt her demon energy intermingling with his soul, and an awareness of her mother's alien world opened his mind to a vista of unimaginable splendour. Yet, it was isolated and apart from the multitude of other cosmic realms. Then he sensed her demon energy consuming his being.

Suddenly, stripped of his human soul, he became a singular point of awareness absorbed in the vastness of cosmic existence.

An unknown source called his name 'E d w a r d.' He was abruptly drawn back into his soul, but it was different and no longer tainted with the demon energy or human conditioning. Only his memories and knowledge remained.

He groaned and found he was back in his body with Pirtsha's sweaty body clinging to him. She was shaking, and he climaxed. For several minutes, they trembled from the deep orgasmic rush that followed.

Then Edward breathed out a satisfied moan as she lifted herself off his spent penis and closed her robe.

'You survived,' she said with immense relief. 'When Lilith absorbed your soul, I thought I'd lost you, but you were repelled. I don't understand why or what happened. Yet, you have changed.'

'I certainly feel different.' He stood, tied his robe, and hugged her.

'I see it in you now. You're becoming an Avatar.'

'Wow!' Sophia stood and rubbed her crotch. 'That made me come, and I've wet myself.' She giggled.

'Me too,' Alex said, and Audrey nodded. She was still panting.

'I think we experienced a group orgasm,' Vincent said, looking embarrassed, and the men agreed.

'I need to clean up and change my pants,' Martin said and chuckled with a shake of his head.

Pirtsha touched Edward's face and gazed into his eyes. 'Your balance has freed me from Mark's conditioning and subdued my demon nature. But you are no longer human, Edward. You understand that, don't you?'

'Yes, I know the sacrifice.' He lowered his head, then smiled at her. 'I have seen the Abyss between the worlds, I've touched the unknowable, and there is no turning back. I also touched your inner being and felt a deep love for you, Pirtsha.'

With a pleasant smile, she clung to him. 'I have never known love before. I will help you find Lucy, and I will never leave you, Edward, never!'

***

Mark sat nursing a brandy in the lounge with his group. They were chilling out, discussing their return to the States and the operation in Washington, but he couldn't get the loss of Pirtsha out of his mind. She belonged to him, and once back, he'd recondition her to erase her free will permanently.

His phone buzzed on the coffee table.

'I have a man for you.' It was Bradley. 'His name is Damon, and he has a score with Edward for busting a terrorist group he was involved with. He's willing to take Edward out and the others if you pay him.'

'Good. I hope he's better than Jonas.'

'Damon won't be in the UK until tomorrow afternoon. I'll bring him around in the evening.' He paused, then asked, 'Anything on Pirtsha?'

'I believe she's with that fucking psychic. And I want her back!'

'Maybe Damon can help.'

'I look forward to meeting this, Damon.' He switched off his phone and frowned. If he could confront Pirtsha, he might be able to reactivate her conditioning to obey him. His gut churned, and he twisted. Sighing, he turned to Luther. 'Has he abducted her and taken control of her mind?' He thumped the table with his fist.

'I can't believe she left of her own accord,' Luther said.

'Which means Edward is a powerful occultist,' Penelope added.

'So, how do we get her back?' Brian asked, stubbed out his cigarette and coughed some phlegm into a handkerchief.

'You know, guys.' Lesley made a half smile. 'Maybe it's karma. You kidnap people to get money. Now Pirtsha has been taken, and you don't like it.'

'Don't make a joke!' Mark snapped at her. 'We need Pirtsha.'

'Would you pay a ransom to get her back?'

'Not while I know where she is.'

'Why don't you go there and talk to her?' Teresa looked bored.

'Interesting idea,' Penelope said. 'We could make contact and find out what's going on.'

Mark sighed, disturbed by the thought of personally confronting Edward. When powerful occultists meet, there is a natural contest over who is more advanced. He shuddered, recalling Edward wounding a Djinn, and frowned. Edward's occult power was growing, and meeting him might not be a good idea. Finally, he reasoned that there were other ways of dealing with him and getting Pirtsha back. He sat back, thoughtfully rubbing his chin.

'Bradley knows someone who will be working with us.' He smiled. 'His name is Damon.'

***

Pirtsha entered the study and found Vincent working on a laptop at the desk. She was about to leave when he stood up and smiled at her.

'What happened to us in that ritual?' he asked.

She frowned at him, sensing his sexual interest in her. 'My mother created a conduit in me to consume souls during sex. I didn't know she was using me like that. Fortunately, Edward used his Serpent knowledge and was released.' She made a little smile. 'The group shared our orgasmic energy because you are all psychically linked to Edward.'

He chuckled. 'That was amazing, but Edward has changed.'

'Yes, when Edward merged with my demon nature, he became an Avatar, a being of the Abyss between the worlds. It was the only way we can search for Lucy in Otherness.'

'Otherness?'

'Dark Matter. Your science knows of it theoretically but has yet to discover its existence.'

'You know of our science?'

'Vincent, I might be a moonchild, but I'm also human, and I've had a lot of time to study the sciences and arts on the Internet.' She tilted her head, sensing his military background and interest in music. 'You like the thrill of danger and classical music. I also like music, Chopin, Beethoven and Mozart.'

His face paled. 'You see into my mind. And you like Chopin!'

'I do like his music, especially the nocturnes.' She smiled at his surprise. 'And I only get impressions from people. I'm trying to get to know each of you.'

'There you are,' Sir John said to Pirtsha and entered the study with Martin. 'Edward is sleeping, and I would like a word.'

'Of course. Edward is in deep meditation to recover from his transformation.' She smiled at them, sensing their interest and concern about her. 'I see you are part of a ceremonial group,' she said to Sir John.

'I suppose you could call it that.' He raised his brow. 'I'm a Master Mason. Though I don't bother with that theatrical malarkey now. Edward has shown us the real McCoy. We have seen beyond this world.'

'What do you want to know?'

'Yes, it concerns our security. You know about Jonas?'

'He was sent to kill your wife and daughter, but he disappeared.'

'I killed him after he shot one of my team,' Martin said.

'You are a warrior. You've been involved in several wars and enjoyed the battles.'

'I have.' He nodded with a smile.

'We need to know about Mark Skully,' Sir John said. 'Just how much of a threat is he to Edward and the group?'

'Mark is seriously dangerous. He will certainly hire someone like Jonas again, and he can conjure deadly beings. Also, he wants you to suffer because you had his brother killed.'

'I haven't had anyone killed!' Sir John looked horrified. 'I never met Skully or his brother.'

Pirtsha sensed he was telling the truth and tried to recall Mark's comments about his brother's death. 'I think it was in America. Mark had scammed the Stock Market, and his brother was involved. I don't know what happened, but his brother was shot, and Mark went into hiding.'

'I remember the scam, and I was living in New York then. But I had no contact with Skully. However, yes, I did help the FBI with the names of people who might have been involved in the scam, and Skully's brother may have been on it or an alias. Then, I returned to the UK. Later, I heard that most people on the list I gave the FBI were disposed of. That happens in America.'

'How can we deal with Skully?' Vincent asked.

'Edward intends to confront him.' She didn't like the idea because Mark was a dangerous man. She frowned, fearing that Mark would come for her and that he would never give up until she was back under his control.

***

Mark viewed Damon in the lounge. He sat opposite in an armchair, smoking a cigarette. The man was in his thirties, dressed in jeans and a blue padded shirt. He had close-set, shifty eyes and dark brown hair. He was a known terrorist and could be a loose cannon.

'Do you know Edward Caster personally?' he asked the man.

'Never met him. After he busted our London cell, they rigged his car but got his wife. I'll make the hit for ya. Who else do ya want done?'

'Three hits, but I want Edward taken out first. Then the others later.' He handed him Henderson's address, and they exchanged phone numbers.

'I'll need to see the place and set it up.'

'Okay, but wait for my call before you make the hit.'

'I don't have time to waste. I'll set it up and let ya know when I'm ready. I'm only here for a week.' He got up, nodded to Mark, then left.

'Can we trust that guy?' Penelope asked. 'I sense his ruthless side, and that bothers me.'

'He will be a good scapegoat when the work is done. Take the heat off us.' Mark closed his eyes, thinking of Pirtsha, and wondered how to get her back and recondition her.

'I got a call from Karl in the States,' Brian said, putting his phone away. He says the Washington operation looks good. He's arranged a safe house for us and a secure place to hold the boy until the ransom is paid. School holidays start in three weeks, and we must be there soon.'

'If it wasn't for Pirtsha.' Mark lit a cigarette and took a deep puff. 'I'd be tempted to head for the States and leave the hits to Damon. The parents are Microsoft billionaires, and the boy is their only son. We're looking to make thirty million dollars on the ransom. More than enough to finish paying for our place in South America and live there in luxury for several years.'

'Why not cut your losses and leave now?' Teresa asked. 'Just how important is Pirtsha?'

'She was my creation, and replacing her will be impossible.' He recalled how Lilith had used him and cringed. 'If I can't get her back, I want her killed.'

'So, what's the plan now?' Luther asked.

Mark shrugged, then sat back, feeling drained from the ordeal. Losing Pirtsha was constantly on his mind.

Chapter Eleven

Sophia kissed Alex. They were relaxing on her bed, enjoying the warm afterglow from making love. 'You are my Jedi lover.' She kissed Alex again and caressed the tattooed roses on her breasts.

'And you are my Star Wars princess.' She cuddled Sophia and then sighed. 'When your dad finds out about us, I'll probably have to leave.'

'No! Daddy knows I like girls and wants me to be happy, but Mumsie is traditional and wants grandkids. She made me date several guys.' She made a face, then smiled. 'You have brought joy into my life.'

'I haven't felt like this for years. I never thought I'd love again. And I like being here.' She raised her brow. 'Have you noticed how Edward has changed since merging with Pirtsha?'

'Yeah. There are times when he seems like an alien, more so even than her.'

'Seeing him in deep meditation gives me the creeps. He sits so still, it's like he's a statue.'

Classical music sounded from downstairs. They looked at each other, hurriedly dressed, and went down to investigate.

Sophia found her father, Pirtsha, Vincent and Audrey in the lounge listening to a Chopin nocturne.

When the music finished, Pirtsha said, 'That's one of my favourites. Certain music can connect the mind with psychic threads that reach deep into dreamtime.'

'You are a source of strange knowledge,' Sophia said.

'My understanding is only a shadow of Edward's knowledge from the ancient Serpent.'

'The Night Side of Eden,' Sir John said. 'The Bible has an edited version of Eden. In the unedited version, there are seven trees of knowledge. Four trees are believed to contain the understanding of time, space, consciousness and wisdom. And the three inner trees contain the ultimate plan for existence. Eden is a divine jewel.'

'Did Eden really exist?' Alex asked.

'Not physically,' Pirtsha said. 'It's in etheric space, not dense matter.'

'Have you been there?' Audrey asked.

'My moonchild DNA and foetus were created in Eden, and then Lilith gave me life, and I came into this world.'

'Came into this world? Were you born like us?' Sophia asked.

'No, I manifested here and drew physical matter over my etheric form. Then, I was incubated for several years until this adult body was fully developed. I never had a childhood or knew what it was like to be young.'

Martin entered with a military tablet. 'Looks like we have a couple of snoops.' He showed them the tablet. 'I caught this guy looking in one of the windows.' There were images of an older man taking photos with his phone and a younger man loitering outside the house. 'I've sent Harry the images. He might find out who they are.'

'Better increase our security,' Vincent said.

Sophia shuddered, hugged Alex, and noticed her father watching them. He raised an eyebrow, looked at Audrey, and then smiled at them with a nod of approval.

***

Mark greeted Bradley when he entered the roof garden with Brian.

'How are things?' he asked, motioning them to sit.

'I face the inquiry in four weeks over accessing those classified files.' He sighed wearily, then shrugged. 'I might jack it in with the force.'

'You can come with us to the States.' He smiled at Penelope, who came over carrying a tray with tea and sandwiches. She placed the tray on the table and sat next to Lesley. 'What about Henderson and Edward?' he asked Bradley.

'Not much. The detective said they stayed inside, and the place was secured with cameras and detectors. He did identify Pirtsha in one of the front rooms, but they spotted him, so he's off the case. As for Damon, he's intent on killing Edward first, then the women.'

'I'm not sure about him.' Mark sipped his tea. 'He's got his own agenda, but he'll make a good scapegoat once we've done and gone.'

'That can be arranged,' Bradley said. 'I know who to contact at the Yard to tip them off about Damon.'

'Mark!' Penelope stood to get his attention. 'Why don't you cut your losses? We can leave for the States and let Damon deal with Edward and Henderson?'

'I'm not leaving Pirtsha there!' He sat back thoughtfully, rubbing his chin. 'I'm going to try to bring her back. We'll use the ritual of overshadowing.'

'A stealth rite should work,' Luther said, twiddling his dangling earrings.

'It will.' Mark finished his tea. 'We'll use subliminal enforcement and conjure a distortion mist.'

'It means entering her Dreamtime,' Penelope said unenthusiastically.

'Could be fun,' Mark said with a big grin.

***

Edward viewed Lucy's body on the bed and wanted to cry. He had failed again to protect the ones he loved. Touching her pale face, he felt the absence of her spirit. Focusing, he psychically scanned her empty mind to find her soul lost in the vastness beyond the Abyss, and his heart ached for her.

'I feel your sadness,' Pirtsha said, touching his arm.

'I don't know if we can find her soul.'

'We will try, but it will mean going deep for days. Time zones are changeable beyond the Abyss.'

'I must ensure the group is safe before we go in for that long.'

'Yes, Mark is still a serious threat.' She frowned, then smiled at him with a sparkle in her eyes. 'I like your group. They have bonded at a deep level with you.'

'They also like you. And so do I.'

'When we merged, I sensed your unhappiness. The loss of your wife and now Lucy.'

'I can still hear the explosion, and her death changed my life. Now Lucy is gone, and the suffering has returned a hundredfold. I must find her, Pirtsha. God knows what happened to her soul. It breaks my heart.'

'First, you must regain your inner strength and complete your transformation into an Avatar.'

'How long will it take?'

'Depends. The deep meditations will hasten the process of integration.'

He closed his eyes and cringed from the agitated internal energies. 'Will you be okay while I meditate?'

'I also need to rest. This has been a traumatic experience for me. You've helped me to break Mark's conditioning and subdue my mother's influence, but I need to internalise the changes. The stresses are wearing me down.'

She leaned in and kissed his cheek softly as he wrapped his arms around her. He enjoyed a sense of comfort holding her close and gently brushing the hair out of her face. Looking into her striking, dark eyes, he could sense the depth of her loneliness and the feeling of not entirely belonging among the others. But despite their differences, he found himself deeply drawn to her unique and otherworldly nature. And when they climaxed in the power rite, he felt an intense, transcendental connection with her that was unlike anything he had ever experienced.

'Who is Lilith?' he asked. 'I've heard of her and experienced her powerful alienness.'

'Mark also wanted to know about her. So I did ask.' She paused. 'No one knew her in this world, yet they had heard and were afraid of her independent nature. Mother and the one who became Adam were created from the progeny of the third causation. By entering Eden, they had to relinquish their divinity and become human. Adam underwent the change, but Lilith refused and uttered the name of the Serpent, which was how she freed herself and was cast out by the aliens who were once the Watchers on Earth. They are long gone now.' She frowned. 'But Mother is far more than any Djinn or demon. In Otherness, she, like the Serpent, is a lawless power to be reckoned with.'

'What do you know of the Serpent?'

'Not much. It's a being from the first creation and the guardian of the God Flame in the Night Side of Eden, which the angels of death protect.'

He frowned at her. 'Angels of death?'

'They exist, and no one, great or divine, can survive against them because their monadic weapons cause the oblivion of your spirit.

'I didn't know that.'

'Mother said they prevented her from entering the Night Side.'

***

While Edward lay in deep meditation, Pirtsha went to her room, showered, and settled on the bed. Her body ached with exhaustion. As she was relaxing, there was a tap on her door, and Vincent looked in.

'Just checking you're okay?' he said with a smile.

'Yeah, I'm just tired.'

'Get some sleep, and you'll feel better. Martin will be on duty for the next four hours. We take it in turns.' He left and closed the door.

Alone, she lay back thinking about Mark and sensed he was up to something, but she felt safe with Edward and his group. Gradually, she fell asleep.

In her dream, Pirtsha stood in an endless, densely wooded park. At first, she enjoyed the atmosphere and serene beauty, but an unsettling feeling grew. Shadowy figures emerged, closing in, and a sense of dread overwhelmed her. With a shock of urgency, she panicked and started to run. Her heart was pounding as she headed for a road she could see in the distance. But looking back, she saw the shadowy figures getting closer and knew she was in danger. Suddenly, everything stopped, and she felt herself sinking into the ground as if trapped in quicksand. The sensation of being sucked under the ground was so intense that she woke up gasping for air, still shaking with fear.

Taking long, deep breaths, she calmed herself and wondered where she was. Her thoughts were scattered and disoriented, like in a dream. Getting up, she dressed. What was she doing here? She had to go, get out, and find Mark. He needed her, and she could sense him calling her name, urging her to leave the house. Brian was outside, waiting to take her home. She left the room and went downstairs.

A muscular man appeared in the hallway. 'Pirtsha. What are you doing? You look pale.'

'I'm going home.' She headed for the front door, but he blocked her.

'I don't belong here.' She narrowed her eyes, raised her right arm and pointed at him while squeezing her hand.

The man gripped his chest, moaning in pain.

'Get out of my way!' She demanded with intensity, and he sank to his knees.

'Pirtsha!' Edward shouted, and she gasped, dropping her hand.

She looked around at Edward and felt the spell dissipate. Then she saw Martin on the floor and helped him up. 'I'm so sorry. I didn't know what I was doing.'

Edward came over and hugged her. 'I was meditating when my wife came to me. Instantly, I knew something was wrong. Are you okay now?'

'I think so.' She sighed. 'Mark got into my dream state and took control of me. I must have let my guard down.' She noticed how pale Martin looked. 'I didn't mean to hurt you.'

'What did you do to him?' Edward asked.

'I used a mudra to stress his heart.'

'Really. Has Skully gone now?'

'Yes, but I felt.' She paused. 'He will kill me if he can't have me back.' She rested her head on his chest, and he hugged her.

'How are you?' Edward asked Martin.

'I'm all right now, but it was like a hand gripping my heart.' He took a few deep breaths and shook his head. 'How did you do that?'

'I think it's part of my demon nature. I'm sorry, Martin.'

'At least you're back with us,' Martin said, sighing with relief.

'I think Brian is outside waiting to take me away.'

They went to the front door and looked out. A taxi was parked across the road with a passenger in the back. Martin gave him the finger, and the cab drove off.

'He will never give up,' Pirtsha said as the door closed.

***

'Lost her,' Mark said, punching the air. 'That bloody psychic broke the spell.'

'How did he break our mist of sleep over him?' Luther asked, rubbing his shaved head.

'I sensed he's changed,' Lesley said with narrowed eyes. 'He's become a powerful occultist.'

'And Pirtsha responded instantly to his command,' Penelope added. 'She broke our spell, not him.'

'I think you may have lost Pirtsha,' Teresa said and stood. 'When we were overshadowing her, I sensed she's broken your conditioning and has control of her demon nature.'

'Is it possible that she and Edward have joined sexually?' Luther asked with a raised brow. 'That may account for her transformation.'

Mark shuddered with a biting ache in his gut. Could Edward have Pirtsha under his control? The thought of her with Edward burned in his mind. If it were true, then she must die.

'I now feel bad about messing with Edward and his group,' Lesley said.

'Let her go. We need to move on—' Teresa started to say.

'I'm not leaving Pirtsha with him!' Mark shouted at her, then calmed himself. 'I still believe I can get her back. If not, I'll deal with her and that fucking psychic.'

***

Pirtsha entered the lounge with Martin. Sir John's cook, Susan, had provided a buffet for their breakfast, and the others helped themselves.

'What happened to you last night?' Vincent asked her.

'Mark and his group overshadowed me to leave the house. Edward broke the spell. They used subliminal magic when I was asleep, and I was caught off guard. It won't work on me again.'

'Any idea what he will do next?' Sir John asked her.

She shook her head slowly. 'He may try again to get me back. If not, he could send one of the dark lords to attack us.'

'Dark lords?' Vincent asked, and his eyes widened.

'Beings that were expelled from this world a long, long time ago. I've seen their fiery pits with Mark. In their confinement, they have become fluidic, energy beings. Quite terrifying.'

'Sounds like hell!' Audrey said with a creased forehead. 'Is Mark that powerful?'

'Yes, he could summon one.' She sensed their concern. 'But he'd need to use his group and perform a power rite. I don't think he will risk it because it's a dangerous ritual, and he's leaving for America soon.'

'The sooner, the better,' Audrey said.

'You said that Edward is an Avatar. What is that?' Alex asked.

'It is a man who embodies an element of the Abyss. We are all bonded to Edward, and he is helping us to evolve beyond our human conditioning.'

'He has opened my eyes to a greater reality,' Vincent said. 'It's like my old life has gone, and I've been born again.'

'He's changed my life, and all of us, I think,' Sophia added.

'I've noticed my sense of awareness has changed,' Alex said. 'I sometimes pick up feelings and thoughts from you guys, especially Sophia.'

'Yes, I feel that too,' Sir John said. 'And the group sessions seem to enhance our psychic awareness.'

'It's like we are family,' Audrey said, then stood when Edward entered.

'How are you?' Pirtsha asked him, tilting her head and sensing his condition.

'Refreshed and complete. And you?'

'Better now you're here. And I see you've mastered the balance.'

'Almost.' He winked at her, then faced the others. 'We must perform a group session to cleanse ourselves and this house. Then I will show you something extraordinary.'

Chapter Twelve

E dward viewed his group waiting for him in the lounge and smiled. 'I see you have bonded and become friends. That is good. My priority is to find Lucy's soul and protect us from Skully. Do you have any questions?'

'We've been in this heightened state since the group sessions,' Vincent said. 'I don't know how we'll feel when it passes and we come down to earth.'

He chuckled. 'This altered state is permanent. It will settle, but you'll never lose this enhanced consciousness.'

'I do feel strange at times,' Audrey said. 'And I don't sleep much now.'

'Nor do I,' Sir John said. 'Mostly, I catnap.'

'I like the buzz,' Sophia said.

Michael, the butler, entered with his wife, Susan.

'Sir,' Michael said. 'Now we understand what is involved. We would like to join the group if that is acceptable.'

'You are most welcome. And it will enhance and protect you,' Edward said. 'Okay, let's form the circle.'

After Pirtsha had energised the group, Edward used an invocation to cleanse them and cast a psychic mist over the property. Then, using an energy spell from the knowledge, he pulled the group into his consciousness and projected out of his body. Like birds, they flew up and out of the Earth's magnetosphere and entered solar space.

Edward took a deep breath and closed his eyes, visualising the ancient garden of Eden in his mind's eye. With a focused intent, he commanded himself and his group to be there. His group expressed some concern as they passed through the turbulent energy barrier. But when they finally entered the garden, they were amazed by the vast, serene paradise with distant mountains and flowing rivers. The sky was a brilliant shade of blue, and the grass was lush and velvety under their feet. Towering trees with colourful leaves rustled in the gentle breeze, and a glistening lake sparkled in the distance.

Beautiful flowers captivated their attention. Each one was unlike any they had ever seen on Earth, with petals that shimmered like precious gems in the sunlight. Marvelling at the beauty around them, a flock of unusual parrot-like birds took flight, their feathers flashing brilliant shades of green, blue, and gold.

Then a long-legged deer strolled towards them, its golden aura shimmering in the sunlight. The group gasped in surprise and delight, unable to believe their eyes. Everything in this magnificent paradise was pristine and beautiful, perfect like heaven.

'Where are we?' Vincent asked, looking around with an open mouth.

'This is Eden. It exists beyond physical space and time,' Edward said. 'The Light Side is in perpetual day, while the other is eternal night. We will depart once you have absorbed the energy from the Light Side.' Edward kept a watchful eye on the group. He could sense their amazement and wonder. Pirtsha approached him with a smile, and he could feel her excitement.

'Mother was banished from Eden by the Watchers of that time. But even they couldn't enter the Night Side. Those Watchers are long gone, and now others come and go to use this place to create the DNA for physical and etheric bodies.' She faced the deer. 'Though I can't enter the Night Side, I love being here.'

'This is a magical place,' he said. 'Can you keep an eye on our group?'

'I will look after them. Here they are like children.'

He watched her join Sophia and the others. Seeing them enchanted with the pristine surroundings, he smiled, enjoying the tranquillity of this realm. Thinking of Lucy, he sighed with a biting ache in his heart. If only she were here to enjoy it. He must find her soon.

The golden deer ambled over and nudged him. Instinctively, he stroked its head.

'You have returned,' the deer spoke in a clear voice. 'Enter the night realm and remember.'

Edward stood still, his eyes closed, as he allowed his mind to drift back to a distant memory. He saw himself as a young boy, standing before the Night Side of Eden. Two mighty angels, their swords ablaze with monadic fire, stood guard at the entrance, but Edward felt no fear as he approached them. The angels stepped aside, pointing their swords downward, allowing him to enter. As he passed through the portal, a sense of foreboding washed over him, and he frowned in remembrance.

He slowly opened his eyes to find himself surrounded by seven towering trees, forming a vast protective circle around a pillar of eternal light. Its brilliance was almost blinding.

Suddenly, a humanoid Serpent emerged from the fountain of celestial energy, and its piercing green eyes focused on Edward. He gasped as he felt the Serpent's holy presence wash over him, but he also knew that this ancient Serpent was a living god from the time of the first creation.

The Serpent spoke to him.

'See and partake of my knowledge. When you understand who I am and why I have empowered you, then you will be transformed.' The Serpent's words touched him with an alien love that flushed his heart and opened his mind to a vista of unimaginable infinity from a time before time. Suddenly, the magnificent trees surrounding him became illuminated with knowledge from the beginning of creation, including the purpose of existence. Edward's senses were overwhelmed. He covered his eyes and trembled as he felt the Serpent's energy flow through him. Gradually, he regained his composure and deliberately closed the door to the Serpent's mind.

Breathing out a deep sigh of relief, he opened his eyes. The Night Side was gone, and he faced a radiant golden deer whose nature shimmered with spiritual love. Edward frowned, realising that encountering the Serpent had profoundly changed him in a disturbing way.

'You are no longer your human self. You and Pirtsha are welcome. However, some of your group are not yet worthy of returning,' the deer said.

'They will change and become worthy,' he replied.□

The deer nodded with a hint of a twisted smile. 'They are ready to depart.'

Edward called his group and made the command to leave. There followed a sensation of being sucked out of that realm and of passing through a turbulent energy barrier, and they were abruptly back in the circle.

'We did it,' Edward said with relief, closed the rite, and breathed slowly, trying to calm the lingering energies from the Night Side. For a long time, the image of that ancient Serpent remained etched in his mind. Pirtsha touched his arm and smiled at him.

'That was heaven,' Audrey gasped.

'And we were out of our bodies as a group,' Sir John said. 'I have never experienced anything like that before.'

'You saw the magical deer,' Pirtsha said. 'It sensed my nature and spoke to me. Asked me where we came from and that we could only visit for a short while.'

'It also spoke to me,' Alex said. 'Told me I have negative karma to work off, then I could return.'

'That's what I got,' Martin said. 'Showed me the people I've killed in the ops and bad things I've done.'

'Me too,' Vincent added and made a face. 'I now understand karma and what must be done to make peace with my soul.'

Susan hugged Edward. 'Thank you, sir. We have seen the paradise of Eden. And the deer showed me how to live a balanced life.'

'The deer told me Edward is our guide and protector,' Martin said.

'I feel transformed from the experience,' Henry added.

'My friends, by experiencing Eden, you have been initiated into the world of the occult,' Edward said and smiled at Pirtsha. 'We are now a team of explorers into the vastness beyond physical space. Yet, we are also friends—one for all and all for one.'

Pirtsha stood and embraced him. 'I will never leave you, Edward, never.'

He kissed her. 'We are the nucleus of this group. And through our bonding, you are no longer conditioned to obey Skully, and you have control over your mother's influence. You are a free spirit and one of our group.' He glanced at the others. 'Does anyone object?'

Sir John clapped his hands and stood. 'I bow before Pirtsha. You are the most extraordinary being I have ever known.'

Audrey, Alex and Sophia stood. 'We, with Susan, are your sisters, Pirtsha,' Audrey said.

'And we are your brothers,' Vincent said, motioning to the men.

Michael, Susan and Henry bowed their heads to Pirtsha. 'We are here to serve you, Madam,' Michael said.

'I am honoured, but I'm just a moonchild.'

'And I am an Avatar from the Night Side of Eden. Together, we are the nucleus of this spiritual group.' He stood and faced them. 'There will be times when Pirtsha and I are away searching for Lucy's soul. And I would like Sir John and Audrey to act as our deputies. You know how to energise the group, and it would be good to practice without me. Pirtsha will help you. With Skully out there, we are still in danger.'

'We must also keep monitoring the property,' Martin said. 'Harry came back with an ID on that guy we had snooping around. He's a freelance terrorist called Damon Micquine and does private hits for money.'

'Micquine!' Edward tensed. 'He could be a relative to Jolon Micquine, whom I helped to bust in London.' Thinking of Glenda, he shuddered, recalling the image of her dying in the burning car. Then he saw Lucy in his mind, and he sagged. How the hell was he going to get her back? The thought of her soul trapped beyond the abyss gripped his heart, and he stifled a sob. He had failed both of them.

Looking at Martin, he said, 'We must be careful.'

'I've got both vehicles fitted with anti-tamper kits and cam eyes.'

***

Mark poured himself a large whisky, sat back in his armchair in the lounge, and closed his eyes. Thinking of Pirtsha, his gut tightened with anger. He would make her suffer for leaving him. But how would he get her back? His phone buzzed. He tensed and took it out. It was Damon.

'The place is tight with armed security,' he said. 'It'll mean waiting for him to come out. I'll take out Edward first, standard fee fifty-k, with twenty-five up front to set up the hit. Then I'll track and do the others later once the dust has settled.'

'Are you sure you can take out Edward? It has to be a clean hit.'

'I can do it, but it means waiting for a positive headshot when he comes out. I've done five successful hits like this, two in the UK.'

Mark rubbed his chin, thinking that if Edward was permanently out of the picture, Pirtsha would be free of his control, and getting her back would be much easier.

'Okay, Damon, I'll have Brian sort the fee. Half now, and the rest when the job is done.'

'I'm staking out the place. It could take a couple of days. Then I'll be around to see you and work out the other hits.'

'Fine.' He switched the phone off.

'You look pleased,' Penelope said. 'Good news?'

'That was Damon.' He smiled. 'He's going to dispose of Edward, and I'll get Pirtsha back.'

'Without him, the rest will fall apart,' Luther said, and Penelope nodded her agreement.

'Edward may not be an easy man to kill,' Lesley cautioned, sitting up in her chair and focusing on Mark. 'He is a practising occultist. And they have armed security there.'

Mark exhaled heavily. Lesley had a keen sense of intuition, and she was right. He would have to be careful dealing with that fucking psychic.

'Damon has a grudge against Edward,' Brian said. 'He'll find a way.'

'Perhaps we should back off to let them feel safe and get careless?' Luther suggested.

'Can you arrange to transfer twenty-five grand to Damon's private account?' Mark asked Brian and then faced the others. 'I think we should check out Henderson's place. But we'll wait for Edward to die. Once we get Pirtsha out, I'll send a morphic entity to wipe them out. They've just pissed me off!'

'Those morphic devils are fucking dangerous, Mark,' Penelope said, narrowing her eyes. 'Are you sure?'

'Yeah, it'll end this mess.'

'Then we can leave for the States and get on with our lives,' Teresa said.

***

Edward left Pirtsha, working with the group and went to see Martin, who was monitoring the security cam-feeds and detection systems in the cloakroom.

'Had contact with Craig,' Martin said, looking up at him. 'He's recovering from his wounds and plans to return to Bristol. He's got his mum and sister there to look after him. The private hospital is costly, but Sir John has paid upfront and has given Craig a generous bonus.'

'I'm glad he's okay.' He looked at the bank of monitors displaying dozens of views inside and outside the property. 'How are things?'

'Everything looks normal. It's quiet most of the time.'

'I feel it's like the calm before the storm,' Edward said, placing his hand on Martin's shoulder and then sighed. 'I want to search for Lucy's soul, but it might mean being gone for days, and I'm concerned about the group.'

'We can look after ourselves.' He made a little shrug. 'Never thought my life could change so quickly and irreversibly. Now, I'm a member of an occult group. How bizarre is that?'

'Do you like the group sessions?'

'It's out of this world, and the buzz is bloody amazing. I like the—'

The doorbell rang, and Martin checked the door cam. A young man was outside with a clipboard. He rang twice, left, and crossed the road to another house.

'Just another cold caller,' Martin said.

'I got some things to do. Then I'll check on Lucy.' Edward left and went to the bathroom. Washing his hands, he thought of his wife. She was the love of his life. Recalling their time together, he smiled at the joy of bringing up Lucy, then felt torn inside. It seemed a long time ago. He tried to connect with Glenda, but the memory faded. He was too upset.

Through a window in the rear hallway, he noticed Susan, Michael and Henry in the back garden having a tea break and went to join them.

'Can we get you anything, sir?' Michael asked and stood.

'No. I just wanted to see how you guys are.' He motioned for Michael to sit. 'Do you like the group sessions now that you're involved?'

'Yes, sir,' Susan said. 'We find the sessions quite magical.'

'And Pirtsha is an extraordinary woman.' Henry grinned. 'She has a presence that er...stimulates certain parts.'

They laughed at him.

Edward's heart skipped a beat as a sudden chill ran down his spine. He quickly turned his head, catching a fleeting glimpse of Glenda from the corner of his eye. She shouted his name and beckoned him urgently. Instinctively, he moved towards her, but a powerful impact to the side of his head staggered him. He stumbled and fell to the ground.

Then he saw Martin burst into the garden and fire two silenced shots at the open window in the empty house.

Martin used his communicator. 'Got a sniper next door, and Edward's been shot. I'm going in.'

Pirtsha appeared and went straight to him. He was lying on the lawn, holding his bleeding head. Then, Susan knelt by him with a first aid kit and examined the wound.

'You were lucky the bullet only skimmed your skull.' Susan bandaged the wound to stop the flow of blood.

'What happened?' Pirtsha asked, almost in tears.

'A sniper got me.' He frowned, trying to ignore the pain. 'Strange thing, I saw my wife over there and moved towards her, else the bullet could have got me between the eyes.'

'Your wife's spirit may have saved you,' Pirtsha said.

He felt Pirtsha place her hands on either side of his head, and her breath was warm on his face.

'You may feel some pain and be unconscious for a while, but I will be here,' she said.

Edward felt a surge of healing energy flood and stimulate his inner being. He moaned with immense relief, looked into her sparkling brown eyes, and passed out.

***

Mark's body tensed as he prepared to anchor a thread into the confinement pits. He focused on the cavernous energy pools, scanning for a spot of concentrated matter where he could attach his anchor thread. After pinpointing a suitable location, he steeled himself for what was to come and shuddered as several ancient beings materialised from the distorted energy fields and confronted him.

One of the grotesque forms addressed him, 'You seek our aid?'

'I need help in my world.'

'You have a gift for the work?'

'Yes, using me as a conduit, you can claim, on their deaths, six advanced human souls for your pleasure.

'Six souls for our amusement. Acceptable,' one of the entities agreed.

'I will return when ready.'

'This anchor will remain for you.' They re-entered the warped energy fields.

He dissipated the energy in the circle and breathed a sigh of relief.

'Did you do it?' Penelope asked, and she made an unpleasant groan.

'Yeah. I'm in.' He felt the anchor point was set and smiled. 'That is one shit place to fuck with.'

'It's an evil cesspool of existence,' Brian said, standing awkwardly. He was shaking.

'There's an unholy brood of beings festering in those depths,' Teresa muttered.

Luther chuckled, rubbing his shaved head. 'And they don't like to be disturbed.'

'That is understood,' Mark said and stood with a smile. He had arranged a gift for the work.

His phone buzzed, and he took it out. It was Damon.

'Got Edward, but I took some damage.'

'Is Edward dead?'

'Yeah, I got a headshot, and he fell. I'm at the hotel being patched up. And I want my fee. You didn't pay the first half. We agreed on fifty-k. Once you pay, then I'll do the other hits.' He disconnected.

'Edward is dead,' Mark told them, feeling relieved. He looked at Brian. 'Damon said you didn't pay twenty-five grand into his account.'

'I didn't because the account wasn't in his name, so I decided to wait.'

'If Edward is dead, then pay him the fifty grand.' He closed his eyes and tried to scan for Edward, but failed.

'Better check out Henderson's place,' Luther said.

'Let's have a break first.' Mark rubbed his head. He was still buzzing from the dark ritual. 'Then we'll see what's going on there. And with Edward out of the way, they'll be in disarray, and I'll get Pirtsha back.'

***

'You need to rest,' Alex told Edward in the study and packed away her medical kit. 'I had to stitch the wound. But you're lucky it was a glancing blow and didn't damage the surface of your skull too much. Might be wise to have it x-rayed.'

'No need. You've done a good job, thank you. Lucky for us that you're a medic.' He looked up as Martin entered.

'He got away, but he's wounded,' Martin told Edward. 'On the monitor, I saw a window had opened in the adjacent house and came straight out, but he'd shot you. I fired twice into the open window, and one hit him. We found fresh blood in the attic of that vacant house. Susan and Sophia are cleaning it up in there.'

'It was close,' Edward said. 'He must have been waiting for some time. I hardly ever go out in the back garden.'

Martin frowned, raising his shoulders. 'After Jonas, I have been checking that place out, but not recently. Sorry about that.'

Pirtsha entered. 'I've shrouded this property in a psychic mist to prevent them from scanning us. They may think you're dead. Mark will have a Djinn looking for you, but your signature has changed to that of an Avatar.' She paused, making a face. 'I feel he might come here to get me. I don't know when.'

'We'll be waiting for him.' Martin nodded to Vincent.

'I would like to do a group session,' Edward said.

'First.' Pirtsha moved behind Edward and placed her hands on either side of his head. 'I want to give you a healing.'

Edward felt the tingling energy flow between her hands and through his head. He made a soft, pleasant sound and relaxed. She had that magic touch.

***

Edward found the group waiting for him in the lounge. Michael, Susan and Henry were also there.

'How are you?' Sophia asked. 'That's a nasty wound to your head.'

'Thanks to Susan, Alex and Pirtsha, I'm on the mend.'

'You were fortunate,' Vincent said with a serious frown. 'The sniper had a clear shot.'

'His wife saved him,' Pirtsha said. 'She distracted him, and he moved just in time.'

'It's true.' Edward touched his head and winced. 'I was careless, and Glenda nudged me.' He sighed. In his mind's eye, he could see her smiling at him. She gave a little wave as the image faded. The thought of Lucy surfaced, and he groaned. Where was she? How could he find her?

'I'll get back to monitoring the security systems,' Martin said, patting Edward on the shoulder.

'Are we doing a group session?' Sir John asked.

'Yes. I want to find out what Skully's up to. Just a projection should do.'

'He'll be scanning us to see what's going on here,' Pirtsha said. 'And he may send someone around.'

Edward entered the circle and sat cross-legged on the carpet with his back straight. Pirtsha stood behind him with her hands on his shoulders. He tensed as the current flowed from her through him and energised the circle.

'Impressive,' he said. 'You have mastered the art of group power.'

'Pirtsha is a good teacher,' Audrey said. 'And we're learning to act as a collective force.'

'I'm going to do a projection, and Pirtsha will use the group mind to allow you to see and hear what I see. Hopefully, it will work.'

As he closed his eyes, he felt himself gradually separating from his physical body. Rising, he hovered above the group in the room, but before he could leave, he saw a figure materialise before him, and he gasped. It was Glenda, his wife. She appeared in her astral body, looking young and radiant, with her long blonde hair cascading over her shoulders and her flowing yellow gown enhancing her shapely form. He was immediately captivated by her beauty and his love for her. They locked eyes, kissed, and embraced.

'I have watched over you and Lucy,' she said.

'I have often sensed you with us and missed you so much.'

'I know, but now you have embraced that dark knowledge to find Lucy's soul. I don't know if you can find her, but I know of your sacrifice, Edward. I will always remember you, our love and our togetherness. But now is my time to move on.'

'No, don't go!'

'I must, and...and this is goodbye, Edward. Sadly, our paths will never cross again.'

He felt an emotional shock flush his being. 'Why?'

'You know the soul's journey, Edward. I will eventually reincarnate. But your path will take you far away. Now, you must find and look after Lucy.'

'You know I will.' He felt her love and mellowed. 'Our time together was wonderful, but it was cut short.'

'It was karma that I had to work off from previous lives. There are no accidents in this world because everything is karmic. You have the knowledge and know this is true.'

He felt she had gained a rare karmic balance and was no longer tied to this world or even to him. 'You have done well. I give you my blessing and wish you well on your journey. I will not forget you.' He felt their love dissipating, leaving a deep sense of spiritual joy.

'You have a new wife now who will take you beyond the Night Side of Eden. Farewell, my love.' She waved, and her astral body dispersed as her soul entered a higher plane of planetary existence.

Bracing his inner being from the emotion of seeing Glenda leave, he focused on Skully's penthouse and was abruptly hovering over the roof garden, where Mark and a group of people were having tea. He moved near to listen.

'There's been no feedback that Edward has died.' Bradley shrugged. 'My source at the Yard says nothing has been reported. No incidents, ambulance or emergency calls.'

'If Damon had shot Edward in the head, he would be dead or in need of medical assistance,' a woman said.

'He told me he got a headshot, and Edward fell.' Mark frowned. 'But did Edward die?'

'We don't know. I called John's landline, and no one answered,' Bradley said. 'And I called his mobile, but there was no answer. They're in lockdown.'

'We need to check out their place, and I'll have a Djinn scan for Edward.' Mark suddenly stood and glanced in Edward's direction.

Edward felt a jolt and was back in the circle.

Pirtsha gripped his shoulders, and he looked up at her.

'How are you?' she asked. 'We saw your wife!'

'Glenda has moved on. I saw her absorbed into the causal plane.'

'She is an advanced human. She saved your life as a gift of her love and wants you to find Lucy's soul.'

'I sensed that too. Glenda merged with me before leaving.' He smiled at her. 'She said you are now my wife because we have bonded.'

'Am I? I would love that, Edward. But Mark will not let me go.'

'He's going to use his group to scan for me.'

'We will be ready.' She hugged him.

***

Mark tapped into the energies of the Abyss and charged his group. When ready, he summoned a Djinn that manifested its shimmering alien form in the room. It made a hissing noise, and its black eyes scanned everyone.

'Is Edward Caster alive?' Mark asked the Djinn and projected Edward's signature.

Ten minutes passed, then the Djinn responded, *'Mists, distortion, difficult to see, human yet not. Here yet not.'*

'That doesn't make sense. Is Edward dead or alive?'

'Uncertain, different.'

Mark gripped the Djinn and focused on Henderson's place, but couldn't enter the property.

'Fucking place is shielded!' Mark shook his head. 'It's only to stop us viewing, but how did they do it, and what is going on?'

'They have Pirtsha there,' Penelope said. 'She could easily use their group to cast cloaking spells.'

'Yes, and she's a skilled occultist,' Lesley added.

'We know she's there, but is Edward alive or dead?' Luther asked.

'Well?' Mark asked the Djinn with a potent command for it to answer.

'Unknown!'

Annoyed, Mark dismissed the Djinn.

'We don't need the Djinn,' Luther said. 'The mist is etheric, and we can use a spiderbot to penetrate.'

'Interesting. I haven't created one since I was a kid.' Mark smiled at the memory of using one to freak out his parents when they wouldn't let him have the money he wanted.

'What's a spiderbot?' Brian asked.

'It's an elemental creature that we create,' Mark said. 'It has limited power but can get through a psychic barrier to see and listen to what's happening.' He chuckled. 'Let's make a spider bot,' he told the women.

'We'll have to grow the spider from your sperm,' Penelope said.

'Hubbell bubble, these witches mean trouble,' Luther chuckled and lit a cigar.

'It'll take a while.' Lesley stood, and the witches gathered around Mark.

It took them three hours to incubate the elemental creature into a visible form.

A dark brown beetle-like shape had formed in a bowl of magical elixir within their circle, and it moved and breathed.

'We have used our spells and fluids to nurse that little bugger into a spider form,' Penelope said, looking pleased.

'Have you anchored it with a name?' Mark asked, prodding the spiderbot, and it whistled.

'Yeah, we tagged the thing,' Teresa said. 'It's called Tosh.'

'Good. Let's use Tosh to spy on Henderson.' He sat and focused his intent, then summoned a group of elementals to infuse the creature with life. As it came alive, its body crawled out of the bowl and headed towards Mark, its donor father.

As Mark shut his eyes, he focused his mind on the spiderbot. He had to be patient in manipulating and using its limited senses, but after some time, he successfully commanded it to enter Henderson's house. The spiderbot passed through the psychic barrier and materialised in the hallway. Moving forward, he found no one there, but as the bot entered the lounge, he saw a group of people gathered around Pirtsha. His gaze fixed on her, and he sensed she had changed. Henderson was standing next to her, and they were engaged in conversation.

'...and seeing his wife was a revelation,' Sir John said. 'But what happened to her?'

'You don't know.' She frowned and puckered. 'When the physical body dies, you exist in your astral body for a certain time before it disintegrates, and your soul passes through mental awareness and rests in a causal form. Glenda will be in that causal state for a long time.'

'Is that what happens to us?' a young woman asked, and he recognised it was Sophia.

'It is, and you've all experienced your inner bodies in Eden.'

A muscular man entered the room. 'Where's Edward?' he asked.

Pirtsha looked around at him. 'He's resting.' Suddenly, her eyes widened, and she pounced, stamping her foot on the floor near him.

'Fuck!' Mark cried out and held his head. 'Pirtsha sensed me and trod on the spiderbot.'

Teresa chuckled. 'She is one savvy woman.'

'Did you learn anything?' Luther asked.

'I got in under their mist and saw Pirtsha, Henderson and his daughter, but Pirtsha spotted the spiderbot and squashed it.'

'You want to try again?' Penelope asked.

'No. She'll be scanning for those bots now.' He paused, clenching his fist. 'Pirtsha said Edward was resting.'

Brian pulled out a pack of cigarettes and lit one. 'Then he is still alive?'

'Damn.' Mark exhaled, gritting his teeth.

***

'What you doing?' Martin asked Pirtsha after she had stamped the floor near him.

'It was a spider probe sent by Mark.'

'Is there any way we can attack him?' Vincent asked.

'Not directly, because he is protected. But...' She smiled. 'The man who shot Edward can be influenced, and he has access to Mark. He hurt Edward, and that is unforgivable. I will ponder on this.' Leaving them, she went to her room and sat in the chair by the bed.

Closing her eyes, she focused her mind and scanned for Damon's signature. Gradually, an image formed of him in a hotel room, sitting by the window. His left arm was bandaged, and he was cleaning a handgun. Moving near, she used the Dark Current to see his thoughts. He was concerned about owing money to the syndicate and was annoyed that Mark hadn't paid him yet. He was a troubled soul who liked to kill but knew it was morally wrong.

'*Mark hates you and will not pay.*' She slipped her energised thought into his mind, and he scowled with a rush of anger. He hurt Edward, and she had to resist the temptation to seriously wound him. Instead, she messed with his reactive mind, set two subliminal commands, and left him to fester.

***

Edward woke from a deep, healing sleep to find Pirtsha sitting on his bed.

'We had a psychic visit from Mark,' she told him with a smile. 'He was using a spiderbot to scan us.'

'What happened?'

'I crushed it.'

'Good girl.' He stood and stretched. 'How are the others?'

'All is well.' Looking at his head, she frowned. 'How is your injury?'

He shrugged. 'It hurts like hell, but it's getting better. I was fortunate.' He thought of his wife and sighed. There was no connection with her now. Only his memories of her remained to comfort him.

'Glenda was a lovely woman with an advanced soul,' Pirtsha said as if picking up on his thoughts. 'When I saw her during your projection, I sensed her freedom. And saving your life from that assassin helped to free her.'

'She said you're my wife now.' He hugged her, enjoying their inner bond.

'Do you want me to be your wife?'

'You know I'm from the Night Side of Eden. And since our merging, I feel we have energetically joined psychically.'

'I feel that too. We're not part of humanity. And I will never leave you, Edward.'

'Then, my lovely Pirtsha, you are my forever wife, and I love you.'

'That makes me feel so good.' She kissed and clung to him.

Then he thought of Lucy, and his heart sank.

'Yes, we must search for her soon,' Pirtsha said. 'Too long, and she may not be able to leave. Her soul could eventually be absorbed by the dragon Djinn.'

He felt Pirtsha's concern. 'I want to probe Otherness and see what we're dealing with.'

***

Mark's phone buzzed, and he took it out. It was Damon.

'Where's my money?' he demanded.

'Edward is not dead. You failed the contract.'

'I shot him!'

'He's still alive.'

'Don't fuck with me! I shot the guy, and I want my money.'

'When I have proof of Edward's death, I will pay.'

'I made the hit, and you'd better pay up!'

'You haven't finished the job. Call me when it's done.' Mark tensed, frustrated and angry with Damon. He disconnected and switched off his phone.

'Was that Damon?' Luther asked.

'Yeah, wants his money for the hit, even though Edward isn't dead.'

'I never trusted him.'

'If he kills Edward, I'll pay him. If not fuck him!'

Brian came over. 'Karl has set up the Washington operation and wants to know when you'll join them.'

'Yeah, that's got a big payout. Better get ready to leave.'

'I'll let Karl know we're on our way,' Brian said. 'And I'll sort out our travel docs.'

'What about Edward and Pirtsha?' Penelope asked.

Mark grunted. 'I'll deal with them. We'll do one more power rite tomorrow, then leave with or without Pirtsha.'

***

'I want Sir John and Audrey to form a circle. Use the invocation Pirtsha taught you to protect yourselves and this place. I'm unsure what will happen when Pirtsha and I enter the Abyss or how long we will be away.'

'Is it dangerous?' Vincent asked.

'Probably.' Edward sighed, concerned at entering the vastness beyond the abyss. 'We'll let you know when we return.'

'I hope you find Lucy,' Sophia said, hugging him and Pirtsha.

'Just stay safe. Skully hasn't given up on us.' He glanced at each of them. 'You have the ability as a group to resist psychic attacks. And watch out for snipers. They can be a real pain.' He touched the wound on his head.

'You take care,' Martin said, patting Edward on the shoulder. Then he faced Pirtsha. 'Look after him for us, please.'

'You know I will, Martin,' she said, taking Edward's arm.

'We're going to use the study and try a short journey into the Abyss,' Edward said. 'Best to keep the room closed until we return.'

'Please be careful,' Sophia said with a worried look.

***

In the lounge, Mark sat fuming over losing Pirtsha. He tensed, gripping the arm of his chair. Part of him wanted to get her, but he didn't want to confront Edward and their armed security. It bothered him that they had dealt with Jonas and Damon. Edward was still alive, and Pirtsha was with him.

'Our travel docs will be ready tomorrow,' Brian told him and lit a cigarette.

'And I have to supervise the operation in Washington,' Mark said. 'It has a big payout. Then we can take a break for a couple of years.'

'I think Bradley is coming with us. He's worried about the inquiry at the Yard.' Penelope helped herself to one of Brian's cigarettes. 'Lesley and Teresa are packing and will be here in the morning.'

'I've also got to get my stuff,' Luther said, twiddling one of his dangling earrings, then looked at Mark. 'I look forward to the ritual tomorrow. Should be interesting using the Dark Current!'

Mark nodded, feeling the bitter taste of defeat. At least he would have the final victory over Edward and Henderson, but he would lose Pirtsha.

Chapter Thirteen

In the study, Edward sat on the carpet in the lotus posture with his back straight, and Pirtsha straddled him with her legs behind his back and arms around his neck.

'I will open the rift,' she whispered in his ear. 'Then we must merge when we enter the Abyss.'

'I feel afraid of the Abyss, and Otherness is so vast, but the need to find Lucy outweighs the fear.'

'You ready?' She kissed him and placed the palms of her hands on either side of his head.

Edward tensed as the Dark Current from the Abyss infused his body. He held her tightly, and they were pulled into the fierce intensity that separated the worlds. The transition was almost painful, and suddenly, they found themselves standing on the windswept Plateau facing the cosmic realm of Otherness.

'Stay close to me,' she said, holding him. 'The wind is strong. Don't let it take you away.' She shuddered as the wind tore at them. 'You have the knowledge, Edward. Now is the time to use it.'

'I understand. We must create an anchor on the Plateau to find our way back.' Edward used the Serpent's knowledge to cast a luminous thread that attached to the dense substance of the Plateau. It was like an extendable cord that he hoped would pull them back to the Plateau and re-enter physical space.

'Now, I will join with you,' she said. 'Do not be afraid.' She moved away, and her demon nature manifested as a dark yet faintly luminous entity. He felt her attach to his back, overshadowing him like a cloak. The sensation was eerie, but he knew she was there to help and protect him.

'That feels rather nice.' He wriggled with the comfort of her intimacy.

'You have a father-daughter link,' she said. 'That will help us locate Lucy.'

Edward focused his attention on his love for Lucy. He held the thread using the Serpent's knowledge, and they leapt from the Plateau. Instantly, they entered the cosmic realm of Otherness, and Edward gasped. The vastness numbed his mind, and the energy rifts of activity were scattered everywhere. This cosmic realm was teeming with life.

'You must hold your link to the Plateau and Lucy,' Pirtsha warned urgently.

'It's confusing.'

'Use the knowledge.'

As he hovered in the vast expanse of dark matter, the only light came from the faint glow of the rifts. He narrowed his focus on his link to Lucy, probing the rifts with his senses. Gradually, his attention was drawn to a specific world within one of the rifts, where he could sense the presence of his daughter. However, the connection was tenuous, and he needed to strengthen the thread and gain a more precise impression of her situation. He could feel her despair and hopelessness, and it pained him deeply. Using the knowledge, he concentrated and locked onto her thread. Now, he faced the daunting task of finding and freeing her from whoever held her captive.

'There, I think that's the one!' He motioned, and they took to flight, gliding effortlessly in Otherness. Eventually, they entered the rift and found an energy world with structures populated by billions of alien beings.

'Can they detect us?' he asked.

'Yes, if we get near them.'

'Are they dangerous?'

'Yes. This is a rift of the dragon Djinn. I will try to mask our presence, and you must use your link to locate Lucy.'

They were hovering over a breathtakingly massive alien city with towering structures, domes, and sprawling pod-like dwellings. The city was bustling with flying machines and strange vehicles, giving the impression of a highly advanced civilisation. He focused on his link to Lucy and followed it down between the colossal buildings while taking great care to avoid detection. They glided over a vast industrial area, where towering pillars of fiery smoke rose from the ground. Eventually, they arrived at a maze of surface and subterranean dwellings. Overwhelmed by the sheer number of streets and tunnels, he shook his head in confusion, trying to decide which one to take.

As he closed his eyes, he could feel the warmth of his daughter's embrace and her love for him. He imagined being with her and let his heart fill with joy. Suddenly, he held a thread that pulled him towards an unknown destination. He followed the thread and found himself descending into a deep underground structure. As he paused to gather his bearings, he sensed his daughter's presence in the lower dwellings. Following the thread led him to a massive, brightly lit, inhabited chamber. There, he saw a dozen Djinn living in the space.

He moved stealthily, scanning the chamber for any sign of his daughter. Then, his heart sank as he saw her soul trapped in a transparent sphere of plastic energy. She was being held captive, like a trophy that the Djinn proudly displayed.

Suddenly, a constriction spike impacted him, and he fell to the ground, surrounded by the Djinn.

'Intruder,' the commanding Djinn snarled at him.

'I have come for my daughter, whom you abducted from my world,' Edward demanded.

'No!' the Djinn roared with an alien burst that shook the place. 'You have come to join her.' He raised an arm and streamed a powerful, containing force.

Edward fought against the constriction net but was securely bound. The Djinn viewed him with amusement.

'What a prize,' the commanding Djinn gloated. 'You will adorn our dwelling until we sell you at the sky market.'

Struggling, Edward was unable to move or use the knowledge. He had foolishly entered their domain and was unprepared. Like Lucy, he was caught, and the net solidified around him.

Suddenly, Pirtsha separated from him and flared with discordant energy as her mother came through her and manifested as a pillar of monadic fire amid the Djinn. The constriction net dissipated, freeing Edward. And she deployed a power spike that staggered the Djinn and sucked on their collective life force.

Lilith communed energetically with the Djinn, and hurting them with her intense presence, she roared angrily, 'How dare you challenge my shadow! Never touch my child again! Or I will destroy you and infest this world with my feeding minions.'

The Djinn subserviently backed away from her fierce, disruptive presence that was gradually consuming them. Edward stiffened, feeling Lilith scanning his life memories. Then, she connected with him, saying, 'My shadow is your companion. The Serpent has awakened you. And if it doesn't consume your being, we will meet in physical space.'

Abruptly, Lilith was gone, and the wounded Djinn staggered, breathing noisy sighs of relief.

'You are Lilith's child!' The Djinn said.

'I am. Now release her soul!' Pirtsha insisted.

'Take it and leave.'

When the containment sphere dissipated, Pirtsha drew Lucy's soul into her being.

Edward could sense Lucy in Pirtsha's comforting spirit and felt immense relief. He had found his daughter and wanted to take her home.

As they were leaving, the commanding Djinn stopped Edward, 'I recognise your signature now. You're a shadow of the Serpent. You and Lilith's child are welcome to return here. I am Keffian, and this is my brood. We didn't take your daughter's soul. We won it in a fighting contest. Let us escort you safely out of our system.'

He accepted Keffian's offer.

Keffian led them out of the cavern and into the alien world beyond. As they glided through the sky, they passed by enormous structures that floated effortlessly in the air and sprawling space stations that hummed with activity. They flew over vast settlements home to billions of dragon Djinn. Suddenly, Keffian zoomed in on one of the outer planets, revealing a dynamic city that bustled with activity. As they continued their flight, they passed over a vast purple terrain where groups of Djinns engaged in strange tournaments and bizarre competitions.

***

Sophia checked on Lucy. Alex was there, setting up a fresh bag on the intravenous drip. And Vincent was sitting by the bed, holding Lucy's pale hand.

'How is she?' Sophia asked.

'Her vital signs are good,' Alex replied. 'But she will deteriorate the longer she's in this coma.' She touched Vincent's shoulder. 'You like her, don't you?'

'I feel for her. She is so young and innocent,' Vincent said. 'I do hope they find her soul, but I fear for her life.'

Sophia nodded, feeling sad. 'Edward and Pirtsha are still in the Abyss. They've been in there since yesterday. When I looked in this morning, they seemed to be in an energy bubble.'

'Pirtsha said they could be there for days because the time scale is different.' Alex made a face.

'Daddy wants us to do a group session.'

'He's getting good at conducting these rites.'

'Yeah, he used to do Masonic rites at the lodge.' Sophia left and went to the study. She viewed Edward and Pirtsha entwined within a cocoon of shimmering energy. They had been unmoving for over a day.

'I hope you guys are all right,' she whispered, then left the room.

In the lounge, she joined the circle. Michael, Susan and Henry were there.

Martin entered. 'I thought I'd join you. I feel a bit on edge. Security is on remote, and the alarms will sound if anyone tries to get in.'

'Okay, let's get started,' Sir John said, sitting on a chair in the centre of the circle with Audrey standing behind him with her hands on his shoulders. 'Pirtsha taught us this power rite. We've used it before.'

***

Mark received a call from Damon. He didn't answer, and Damon left an angry voice message.

'I'm waiting for you to pay up. I'll do another hit if Edward is still alive, but you owe me the money. Don't fuck with me over this, Mark, or you'll regret it!'

He deleted the message and blocked Damon's number. He didn't like that he was a terrorist and had failed to kill Edward.

'We are ready,' Luther said.

Mark stood and followed him into the lounge, where Brian, Penelope, Lesley and Teresa were waiting. He sat in his armchair, and they gathered around him.

'I feel nervous,' Teresa said. 'Summoning one of those ancient beasts is playing with fire.'

'I feel excited.' Brian chuckled.

'You know the beast will also kill Pirtsha,' Lesley said, wide-eyed.

'She deserted us to be with that fucking psychic,' Mark retorted. 'I can't waste any more time on her. Let's begin.'

The air was tense as the witches and men began invocations, each calling out their commands and summoning the appropriate energies. The circle slowly began to glow with an otherworldly light as the energy built and swirled around them. After twenty minutes of chanting, the circle was finally fully charged and ready for Mark to use his thread anchored in the containment pits and summon one of the beings.

Suddenly, a morphic entity emerged from the discordant energy fields, taking the form of a hideous, fluidic dragon with glowing red eyes that burned fiercely. The entity connected with Mark and demanded a gift for the work to be done.

Thinking clearly, Mark projected an image of a group of advanced souls, including Edward and his companions, and offered them up as a gift. However, the entity must use Mark as a conduit to abduct them. The entity agreed to the deal and would keep them as pets.

For a brief moment, the morphic entity manifested in the room, empowering the circle with its alien being. Then, Mark gripped it tightly and commanded it to enter Henderson's house.

Mark was attached to its back as the entity moved through the house with its crushing alien presence. It entered the lounge, where a group of shielded individuals were huddled together. In the study, Mark found Edward and Pirtsha entwined on the carpet, completely unaware of the threat surrounding them.

Mark focused on Edward and Pirtsha. 'Kill them all,' he commanded.

***

Edward felt a call from Sophia and joined with Pirtsha.

'They need us!' he said.

'Make the connection to withdraw!' she insisted urgently.

He focused on his link to the Plateau and was swiftly pulled there. Holding Pirtsha, he ordered them to return, and they abruptly entered their physical bodies.

Suddenly, he gasped from a crushing weight constricting his body. He stood awkwardly, stretching his back and limbs. A deep buzzing sound from the lounge was making it difficult to think.

Pirtsha took his arm, and her energy eased the pressure on his mind. Then, Sophia's desperate psychic call registered again, and they entered the lounge to find an amorphous dragon-like entity hovering over their group. It was crushing them with its alien energy.

'Protect the group,' he told Pirtsha.

'I'll join them, but Mother can't help us in this world. What about you?'

Clenching his fists, he closed his eyes and focused on the Serpent's knowledge to deploy a protective barrier between him and the entity. With Pirtsha in the circle, he opened his eyes to find the luminous entity looming over the group, releasing destructive surges of crushing intensity.

Suddenly, a powerful burst of its alien energy impacted Edward, and he was thrown against the wall. He cried out from the pain and started to stand when another crippling impact threw him violently across the room. Urgently, he drew a mirror spell from the knowledge, and the following crushing impact was reflected back at the attacker. As the entity reeled, he passed the mirror spell to Pirtsha in the group, and she used it to reflect the attacks.

As the entity broke away from the group, it transformed into a colossal humanoid being, with Mark's projection clinging to its back. It was a formidable sight to behold, towering over everyone. Then, the entity deployed a power spike that sent energy splinters throughout the room.

'Kill him!' Mark's voice boomed, commanding the entity to attack.

Edward tensed as he felt his thread to the ancient Serpent. The entity lunged forward, ready to strike, but suddenly halted and gasped. 'Shadow of the Serpent,' it muttered.

'Kill him!' Mark bellowed again, his voice filled with urgency and malice.

But the entity hesitated. 'Not wise risk wrath of Serpent!' it declared.

'So, we meet at last,' Edward said, his gaze fixed on Mark.

'You have interfered for the last time, and now you die!' Mark thrust a power spike at him.

Edward staggered from the hit but managed to absorb the pain. He mirrored the second spike back at Mark, and the two became entangled in a fierce battle of wills. Mark started to gain control, and Edward realised he was using the entity's energy to fuel his spikes, making them deadly.

Gathering all his strength, Edward raised the palm of his right hand and, using the power of the Serpent, he unleashed a discordant energy spike at the entity. Mark faltered, and the entity reeled, poised to recover and attack again. But before it could do so, Edward sent another spike of the Serpent to drain its energy, and the impact sent it back into the pits from whence it came. With the entity and Mark gone, the room fell silent. Edward breathed a sigh of relief and sank to his knees, depleted.

***

Mark fell off his chair, and his group was in disarray.

'What the fuck just happened?' Luther asked, holding his sweating head.

'He fucking repelled us!' Mark said weakly. 'He sent it back to the containment pits.'

'Fuck! That's it,' Penelope said, standing. 'I'm out of here.'

'Me too,' Brian said. 'I nearly shit myself when it was repulsed.'

'Edward just kicked our arse like he's a fucking dragon master,' Luther said, scowling at Mark. 'Let's get off to the States and forget this ever bloody happened!'

After much hesitation, Mark finally gave in. Edward had banished the mophoric entity from the physical world, and in its desperate attempt to hold on to something, it dragged Mark to the edge of the pits. Although the entity tried to keep him as a pet, Mark desperately severed their connection and repelled the entity's grasp with an occult spike. The experience left him in a weakened condition, and he knew he could never venture into the confinement pits again without risking his life.

'Fucking wiped me out.' Mark stood unsteadily and wiped the sweat from his face. His hands were shaking, and he was physically weak. 'You guys get off. I've got some things to sort out here. Then I'll meet you at the airport in a couple of hours.'

***

Edward felt relieved. He and Pirtsha had returned just in time to expel the intruder.

'It was terrifying!' Sophia said. 'And I kept calling Edward for help with all my being.'

'It was a demon from hell!' Audrey was shaking. 'I've never been so afraid.'

'I can't believe what happened,' Alex said, and Sophia hugged her. 'I felt we were being crushed to death by that thing.'

'It was a monster sent to kill us,' Sir John added. 'How did you get rid of it?'

'During our encounter with the dragon Djinn, Pirtsha's mother intervened with an energy burst that I recognised from the Serpent's knowledge. I used a similar burst on that beast.'

'When we registered Sophia's call, we returned in a hurry,' Pirtsha added.

'What about Lucy?' Sophia asked.

'Pirtsha has her,' Edward said, feeling a warm glow of immense relief.

They went to Lucy's bedroom and stood by the bed. Pirtsha placed the palms of her hands on either side of Lucy's head for several minutes.

Suddenly, Lucy's body jerked and groaned. Pirtsha stepped back, and Lucy opened her eyes. She seemed confused, frowning for a long time. Then she looked at Edward and gasped with delight.

'Dad.' She reached for him. 'Thank you and Pirtsha for getting me out of that horrid place. They tormented and teased me like a pet. I'm so glad to be back here.'

Edward hugged her, and his tears of joy flowed unabated.

'I thought I'd lost you forever.' He kissed her forehead repeatedly. 'I thank God that we got you back.'

***

'If you want to join the others, I can stay and hand over the keys when the agent arrives,' Bradley said to Mark. 'I have things to sort out at home, and I'll meet you in the States later in the week.'

'Thanks, Bradley. This has been a shit operation.' He sighed, rubbing his head. 'I had Brian transfer a hundred grand into your Swiss account for your help. Now I want to get away from the UK.'

'What about Pirtsha?'

'I've not finished with her or the others. When I'm in the States, I'll hire one of the syndicates to hit Pirtsha, Edward and Henderson. I'll let them have a few weeks to drop their guard first.'

'Best way, it'll cost, but they'll do the job.'

He looked at his watch. 'I'll call a cab. The flight leaves in a few hours.' He made the call, then went to pack. Thinking of Pirtsha and Edward, he experienced a hot flush and gritted his teeth. They would have to die, and Henderson.

His phone buzzed, and he answered the call. The taxicab was on its way. He pulled on a coat, picked up his suitcase, and then looked in at Bradley, who was using his laptop in the lounge.

'I'm off now.'

'Have a good trip, and I'll see you in a few days,' Bradley said, returning to using his laptop.

Looking out the window, Mark saw the taxicab parking outside and went down.

As he left the building, his phone buzzed, and he took it out. It was Brian.

'Hi, Mark. We're at the airport, and our flight leaves in ninety minutes. Also, Lesley has decided not to come to the States until she feels better. Anyway, better get a move on if you want to join us.'

'Okay, I'm on my way—' He stopped, sensing a chill of danger and turned to find Damon behind him with a handgun pointing at his head.

'No one fucks with me, shithole!' he said as he fired the gun.

***

Edward hugged Lucy in the lounge. 'I thought I'd lost you.'

'I was trapped in hell. Couldn't do anything.' She rested her head on his chest. 'At least it's over, and I'm thrilled to be back, but you have changed, Dad.' She looked up at him. 'You made the sacrifice to save me, didn't you?'

He exhaled, and a chill gripped his alien heart. 'Yes, I have embraced the Night Side of Eden.' He caressed her face with his fingertips, thrilled she was with him again. 'And I have a new companion, Pirtsha.'

'I like her. She is a strange lady.' Lucy cuddled him. 'When I was in her consciousness, she showed me what had happened here and that someone shot you!'

He cringed and nodded. 'Yeah, I'm okay now.' He showed her his head, and she gently examined the stitched wound.

'You were fortunate, Dad. That could have been fatal.'

'Glenda saved me. Your mother appeared and called me just as the sniper fired.'

'Wow! And Pirtsha said Mum has attained freedom from this world.'

'Yes. Glenda came to me before leaving. It was during a group session, and the others witnessed her appearance.'

'I wish I had seen her.' Her face sagged with a curled lip.

'We still have the memories of her loving spirit.' He brushed a tear from her eye.

'We do. And I will never forget her.' She sighed. 'It's just wonderful to be back here with you. It was a nightmare in that dragon world.' She moaned with a shudder.

Pirtsha came over smiling. 'How are you?' she asked Lucy.

'I am fine now, thanks to you and Dad.'

'I had to merge your soul with mine to bring you back. And you have absorbed some of my nature.' She glanced at Edward, then faced Lucy. 'You now have the shadow of a moonchild in your soul, and we are connected.'

Lucy gasped. 'You are my mother now!' She hugged Pirtsha with tears in her eyes.

'You have been reborn with my spirit,' Pirtsha said. 'And the experience in the dragon rift has enhanced your being. You are very special, Lucy. Like your dad.'

Epilogue

That evening, Edward entered the lounge with Pirtsha to find the others watching the television over the fireplace.

'Look at this.' Sophia turned the sound up.

The newswoman was talking. 'A man was shot dead outside a block of flats in London this afternoon. He has been identified as Mark Chandler. The assailant then shot himself.'

The taxi driver appeared being interviewed in the street.

'I was waiting for my fare. He came out talking on his phone and was shot. He fell, and the man with the gun just stood for several minutes. He looked confused by what he'd done and was muttering or praying. Then he knelt, there were tears in his eyes, and he put the gun to his head and fired.'

'That's Skully,' Sophia said, pointing to an image of Mark Chandler on the screen. 'I wonder who killed him?'

'Who cares?' Alex shrugged.

Pirtsha put her hand to her mouth. 'Mark must have been caught off guard. Others have tried to kill him.' She paused. 'Oh, Edward, this was my fault.'

'What do you mean?' Edward frowned.

'When that man shot you, I was so angry I used the current and spiked his subconscious with hate for Mark and himself. I was concerned he would try again to kill you and wanted to stop him. But I'm...I'm not sorry they're dead.'

'So why did he shoot himself?' Sophia asked.

Pirtsha lowered her head and sighed. 'In case he couldn't get to Mark, I placed the idea of suicide in his reactive mind to pay for his sins. I didn't think of the consequences. I was afraid he would try again and wanted to stop him.'

Vincent raised his brow. 'Whatever you did, Skully and his hitman are dead, and I'm impressed.'

Edward hugged her. 'You may have influenced him, but he chose to do it.'

'So, are we safe now?' Audrey asked.

'I think so.' Edward closed his eyes and used his psychic awareness to scan the penthouse. It was empty. 'Let's do a healing rite? It would be good to have a group session, and Michael, Susan and Henry can join us if they want. They are members of our family.'

'We are like a coven, aren't we?' Audrey said with a wide smile.

'Yes, I can feel we are like a family,' Lucy said. 'Sophia's abduction has brought us together.'

Vincent faced Lucy with a broad, boyish smile. 'It is lovely to see you back with us, Lucy. We were so worried about you.'

'It's wonderful to be here, Vincent, and I see you have changed.' She gave him a little hug, and he blushed.

'Do we, as a group, have a future?' Audrey asked.

Edward smiled. 'You have seen Eden, and that was the beginning of our journey into the mysteries of existence. Pirtsha and I embody the energy of the Abyss, allowing us to function in the worlds beyond. And these journeys will accelerate your evolution and enrich your souls.'

'After that sniper shot Edward,' Audrey said. 'I didn't feel comfortable here, but now Skully is dead, we should be all right.'

'Best to let the dust settle,' Edward said. 'I think it would be good to chill out for a while to recover.'

'I have two islands and a yacht in the Caribbean,' Sir John said. 'Why don't we have a holiday in the sun?'

'I would like that,' Edward said. 'How about the rest of the group?'

Lucy smiled at Vincent. 'I would love that. Living in the sun sounds wonderful after what we've been through.'

'Sounds great to me,' Martin said with a big smile.

'Me too,' Alex agreed, holding Sophia's hand.

Vincent nodded eagerly and looked at Lucy. 'It could be fun?'

'Would you require a butler, a cook and a chauffeur on these islands, sir?'

'Of course, everyone is welcome,' Sir John said. 'You are our friends and part of the group.'

'I think having a long break would be a good idea,' Edward said, hugging Lucy. He sensed her interest in Vincent and raised an eyebrow. She nodded, kissed his cheek and cuddled him. He chuckled and faced Sir John. 'We need to be free from outside influences. What are these islands like?'

'The larger island has a settlement of about sixty native residents. It's mostly a fishing community. There are some shops and a runway for light aircraft. The smaller island is uninhabited and has an old Christian monastery we use when staying there.'

'That would be perfect, John.' Edward gave him a nod of approval, then turned away and closed his eyes. From the Night Side of Eden, the ancient Serpent connected with him. Shuddering with an icy chill, he understood why the Serpent had empowered him to be its dark shadow outside Eden. He was now aware of the Eye of the Serpent living through him symbiotically. Then Pirtsha touched his arm, and in her eyes, he experienced the dynamic presence of Lilith living symbiotically through her. He smiled, and her thoughts entered his mind.

'As I am the shadow of Lilith, so you are the shadow of the Serpent. In these forms, we are together. Now, we can live through these empowered beings. And, we have the power to do whatever we want.'

'True, but we are also independent spirits. We have free will and a universe to discover. With our group, we'll explore the wonders of Otherness. This is our time, Pirtsha. Let's enjoy our freedom and celebrate with our friends.'

'I like that. And our child will be a unique being.' She rubbed her stomach.

'Child?'

She just smiled.

END

About the author

During my youth, I lived in a haunted Victorian house that inspired my fascination with the supernatural. In my early years, I studied various world religions, spiritual paths, and belief systems in an attempt to uncover the meaning of life. Eventually, after growing weary and abandoning my long search, a profound realisation occurred that transformed my understanding of everything.

Years later, after experiencing numerous bizarre paranormal events and gaining some interesting insights, I began writing fantasy stories that incorporate elements of the occult and spirituality. I aim to entertain and inspire others to explore the strange nature of our extraordinary existence.

Life on Earth is a beautiful learning adventure and a playground for the soul, yet it differs significantly from cosmic reality. Those who recall our origins beyond this planet can appreciate how enchanting and occasionally bittersweet physical life can be.

David (dbm)

Also, by this author:

GRIMOIRE The haunting of Rickland Manor

Gavin purchased the Victorian property as a promising investment and moved in with his American girlfriend, Cynthia. When their friends Sally and Raul came to stay for a few days, Gavin took them on a tour of the house. In the dimly lit cellar, they discovered a bricked-up door behind one of the wine racks. Intrigued, they spent several hours working to open it.

Inside, Gavin switched on the lights, revealing a spacious, empty room illuminated by fluorescent lighting. Two large, red outer circles, surrounding a black pentagon, were inlaid in the marble floor. The dusty, stale air thickened around them as they entered the room. Cautiously, they were drawn toward a dark, arched alcove that emitted a faint, humming magnetic energy, which intensified as they approached.

Unknowingly, their presence had triggered the awakening of an ancient grimoire rite that had remained dormant for years. As they left that secret, eerie room, they were unaware that they had become ensnared in an occult web where the physical and supernatural realms were dangerously entwined.

SHARED RECALL The law of the ONE

When two strangers meet by chance, they begin to recall a life they shared before the biblical flood. Byron, a single parent with two children, and Silvie, a gay schoolteacher in a relationship with Grace, embark on a journey to explore these vivid shared memories. Their past as lovers during that extraordinary life complicates their current relationships. Suddenly, an ancient adversary they encountered during that turbulent period re-emerges with deadly intent, dramatically altering their lives forever.

JEWEL in the LOTUS The Lisbeth Project

Jack was still emotionally devastated by the sudden death of his young wife. The accident occurred in America while he was lecturing at Oxford University. When he was offered an assignment as an AI consultant for the Lisbeth Project at the Turing-Minton Institute, he accepted it, hoping that immersing himself in advanced technology would provide a distraction and, ideally, help him gain a sense of closure. However, he was unaware that the project involved working with a mysterious jewel known as the Q-chip, which possesses a unique property called quantum plasticity. As Jack becomes increasingly engrossed in his work on the project, he develops deep feelings for Lisbeth. Then, an incredible twist occurs, allowing him to communicate unexpectedly with his deceased wife.

May you all, in your own way, discover the spirit of freedom.

For those interested, you can visit my website: https://artdaja.com/